THE GHOSTS
OF
RANCHo ESPANTO

"Adrianna Cuevas has written a book that is a beautiful gift to the memory of her father, filled with love and a great respect for the culture and folklore of Cuba."

—Ruth Behar, author of Pura Belpré Award–winning *Lucky Broken Girl* and Sydney Taylor Notable Book *Letters from Cuba*

"A harrowing and important read. Cuevas explores an often-hidden moment in Cuban American history with heart, compassion, and authenticity."

—Ernesto Cisneros, author of Pura Belpré Award–winning *Efrén Divided*

"*Cuba in My Pocket* is an expertly written, emotional roller coaster you don't want to miss."

—Saadia Faruqi, author of *Yusuf Azeem Is Not a Hero*

★ "Inspired by stories from her father's childhood, Cuevas' latest is a triumph of the heart . . . A compassionate, emotionally astute portrait of a young Cuban in exile."

—*Kirkus Reviews*, starred review

★ "Cuevas' intense and immersive account of a Cuban boy's experience after the failed Bay of Pigs Invasion brings a specific point in history alive."

—*Booklist*, starred review

★ "Cuevas packs this sophomore novel with palpable emotions and themes of friendship, love, longing, and trauma, attentively conveying tumultuous historical events from the lens of one young refugee."

—*Publishers Weekly*, starred review

PRAISE FOR
THE TOTAL ECLIPSE OF NESTOR LOPEZ

2021 Pura Belpré Honor Book
NYPL Best Book of 2020
2020 Evanston Public Library Great Books for Kids
Recipient of the Sunshine State Young Reader Award

"A marvelous, magical mystery that deftly blends family, friends and folklore."

—David Bowles, author of Pura Belpré Honor Book and Walter Dean Myers Honor Book *They Call Me Güero*

"Mystery, adventure, humor, friendship, and . . . talking animals—*The Total Eclipse of Nestor Lopez* has it all! Readers will love this funny, fast-paced, heartwarming story."

—Celia C. Pérez, author of the Pura Belpré Honor Book

The First Rule of Punk

"A charming and vibrant debut fantasy."

—*Kirkus Reviews*

ALSO BY ADRIANNA CUEVAS

The Total Eclipse of Nestor Lopez

Cuba in My Pocket

El eclipse total de Néstor López

Con Cuba en el bolsillo

THE
GHOSTS
OF
RANCHO ESPANTO

ADRIANNA CUEVAS

Farrar Straus Giroux

New York

To Heather and Rob
and the magic of Ghost Ranch

Farrar Straus Giroux Books for Young Readers
An imprint of Macmillan Publishing Group, LLC
120 Broadway, New York, NY 10271 • mackids.com

Our books may be purchased in bulk for promotional, educational, or
business use. Please contact your local bookseller or the Macmillan
Corporate and Premium Sales Department at (800) 221-7945 ext. 5442
or by email at MacmillanSpecialMarkets@macmillan.com.

Library of Congress Cataloging-in-Publication Data is available.

First edition, 2023
Book design by Samira Iravani
Printed in the United States of America by
Sheridan, Brainerd, Minnesota

ISBN 978-0-374-39043-3 (hardcover)
1   3   5   7   9   10   8   6   4   2

CHAPTER 1

"**YOU MEANDER DOWN** an empty corridor, late afternoon light streaming through the large, smudged windows," Beto whispers behind me and Yesi as we walk down the hall. "You slowly make your way to the large banquet hall, empty of revelers."

Beto, Yesi, and I stop at the doorway of our school cafeteria at Heron Glade Middle School. Beto gives me a confident smile, his braces glinting in the light.

He puts one hand on my shoulder and one hand on Yesi's shoulder. "Your clan has been granted one item from the banquet hall to aid them in their travels. What do you decide to take?"

Yesi looks at Beto and winks. I swallow hard. "Are we really doing this?" I ask. My ears hurt from straining to listen for approaching teachers or custodians catching us in the act.

Beto squeezes my shoulder as Yesi nods. "Oh yeah. Our clan elects to take the slushie machine," she says.

Beto smirks. "Excuse me, brave traveler. The what?"

Yesi squints, thinking. "The . . . magic fountain of icy sweetness."

"Ah, the magic fountain." Beto nods. "Excellent choice. Roll, please."

Yesi pulls a green twenty-sided die from her jeans pocket. We crouch on the ground, and she flips the die on the gray concrete floor. It tumbles with a clatter that echoes through the hall. Our game is based on Beto describing a situation, Yesi and I deciding what we want to do, and then someone rolling a die to see if we'll be successful. The number that pops up will tell us whether our attempt to steal the slushie machine will work. The higher the number, the better.

"Sixteen," Yesi says.

Beto winks at us. "I see success in your endeavor."

We creep into the cafeteria, our eyes on the gleaming metal prize in the corner of the room.

Beto, Yesi, and I have been obsessed with the role-playing game The Forgotten Age since the beginning of third grade. Other players have come in and out of our game, since it doesn't really work with only three people, but they always lose interest. We're the only ones who've stuck with it for nearly four years.

Last week, my dining room table was covered with our character charts, a Land of Eldervorn map, multi-colored twenty-sided dice, and a thick players' book for The Forgotten Age, brimming with sticky notes. That was when Beto came up with the Great Big Idea to take our characters on a real adventure, one that would make our regular tabletop journeys seem like two-dimensional snooze fests. Beto insisted it was the perfect opportunity to showcase our characters and skills. Yesi agreed immediately. She's the rogue in our group and always pushes our team into dark dungeons and crumbling castles during our adventures. I immediately thought it was a bad idea and wished I could distract Beto's grand plan with the quesitos Mom always baked for us while we played.

But then I remembered Mom hadn't made her famous cream cheese puff pastry treats for weeks. She hadn't done much at all the past few months, actually. And taking our game out of my house meant being away from Dad's grumbling about my grades slipping and Mom's whimpering every time she moved.

We finally agreed that the Great Babosan Trio, as Beto and Yesi had named us, would go on our adventure in the halls of our middle school the last week of sixth grade before summer break. Not only did my gut tell me this latest plan was a bad idea, I still disagreed with our group name, Babosan, since it sounded way too close to the Spanish word for someone who drooled all over themselves.

Beto, Yesi, and I gather around the slushie machine pushed in the corner of the cafeteria, next to the empty vegetable cart that students ignore to get in line for the frozen goodness. My stomach flip-flops at the thought of being discovered by a teacher or cafeteria worker. I squeeze my eyes shut, but all I see are Mom's trembling hands with thin skin and purple veins as she tries to open a bottle.

I shake my head, flinging the image from my mind. "Let's do this," I say. "What's next?"

Beto looks at Yesi and me. "Travelers, you have entered the banquet hall and selected the magic fountain of icy sweetness. Now you must extract the fountain from the castle safely without alerting the guards. What spell will you choose to execute your mission?"

Yesi shrugs. If she had her choice, she'd ride the slushie machine straight out of the cafeteria, whooping and hollering the entire time.

I bite my lip. "I choose a cloaking spell to conceal our treasure from those who . . ." I raise my eyebrows. "Well, like, from Principal Khouri, obviously."

Beto nods. "Ah, from the usurpers who wish to see your endeavor fail."

"Yep, definitely them," I reply, pulling from my backpack a long, flowy pink skirt that belonged to Mom before it got too big for her. I slide it over the top of the slushie machine, the elastic waistband straining, and shimmy it down to the metal cart the machine is perched on. Yesi unzips her blue Miami Marlins baseball hoodie and wraps it around the machine, pulling the hood over the top.

"The spell is complete. You have successfully transformed the magic fountain into a lovely maiden," Beto tells us.

I snort and roll my eyes.

Yesi winks. "Rafa, you can take this maiden to the beach this weekend."

"She will return to her true form once she is freed

from the castle," Beto says, shaking his head. "Also, she doesn't like sand."

We slowly move the slushie machine across the floor, its flowy fabric catching on the wheels. Beto yanks the bottom of the skirt up.

"Hey, careful with the maiden," Yesi says.

I peek out of the cafeteria, making sure we don't run into a custodian, a teacher, or Principal Khouri. Luckily, it's the last week of school and most employees have been zombie-walking right behind the students the moment the final bell rings. I've been staying in the library after school until the librarian kicks me out and makes me go home, something she's been doing earlier and earlier each day.

"The dungeon masters are exhausted from their long day of torturing peasants and have all retired to their quarters," Beto says.

"Huh?" I look at Beto, scrunching my eyebrows together.

"The hallway's clear, bro."

Yesi pushes the cart down the hall as Beto holds the skirt up. I scan the hallway, praying no one sees us. What if Principal Khouri has a secret dungeon below the school where she strings students up by their toes over pits of mutated piranhas? What if the slushie machine suddenly explodes, plastering our kidneys, intestines, and shriveled brain bits all over the windows?

We roll the cart toward the side doors at the end of the hallway. All we have to do is make it out the doors and then we can roll the slushie machine down the sidewalk, across the street, and into the record books of The Forgotten Age. As long as the slushie machine doesn't careen out of control, knock me over, and crush me under its metal weight, putting me in a full body cast for summer vacation.

The hallway slopes down before the doors, the floor covered with bumpy plastic circles to keep kids from gaining too much speed as they launch themselves out the door after the last bell rings. The slushie cart starts to speed up as we slide down the ramp, the wheels echoing loud clacks through the hallway.

"Ño! Beto, it's going too fast!" I hiss as the wheels catch on the pink skirt, tearing the fabric. The ruffles wrapped around the wheels don't slow the cart down. It barrels toward the door. I stick my foot in front of the wheels in an attempt to stop it. All I get is a sore toe as the cart bumps over my foot, continuing its race down the ramp.

"Ah, babosan bomb! We've got to stop it!" Yesi shouts. Any hope of sneaking down the hallway is shattered as her voice bounces off the windows. I watch for the glass to crack as she shrieks our catchphrase.

I try to jump in front of the cart as it careens toward the doors but end up pushing Beto over in the process. He falls to the ground and the cart runs over his hand. He yelps and clutches his fingers to his chest as he scrambles up to join Yesi and me in our race after the runaway cart. Yesi reaches out, and her fingers hook the blue hoodie as it flaps behind the cart barreling down the hall.

But it's too late.

The slushie cart maiden, her skirt torn, bursts through the large blue door and speeds down the sidewalk, only coming to a stop when it crashes into a car bumper.

Principal Khouri's car bumper, to be exact.

Her bumper that is currently three feet below her frowning face and crossed arms.

I put my hands on my knees, trying to catch my breath. My purple twenty-sided die tumbles from my pocket and clatters across the sidewalk. Principal Khouri holds the die with her pointy black shoe, stopping it on one.

Chance of success? Unlikely.

CHAPTER 2

SOMETIMES PARENTS ARE creative when they punish you. Maybe making you squeeze into the same shirt as the little brother you're fighting with.

Other times they're tired and just go for the usual no phone, no video games, no internet.

Dad didn't bother with a traditional punishment. He skipped right over creative, too, since I'm an only child. He blasted all the way to completely unhinged and bonkers.

That's the only way I can explain why I woke up to the smell of poop. I'm not in Miami anymore. I'm in Middle of Nowhere, New Mexico.

Do you know how far away New Mexico is from Miami?

This must be Dad's version of shooting me to the moon to punish me.

When Principal Khouri told him what Yesi, Beto,

and I did with the slushie machine, the vein in Dad's forehead started to pulse and twitch like the boa constrictors people let loose in the Everglades. He pinched the bridge of his nose and hung up his cell phone. Mom just shuffled to the bedroom and went to lie down, ignoring his incoming tirade as she wrapped her bata de casa around her thin frame. Dad's lips formed a tight line as he tried to keep his voice down, hissing at me as he closed the bedroom door where Mom was about to sleep. His thick black eyebrows pressed together like jousting caterpillars.

Between "How could you?" and "¿Qué demonios estabas pensando?" he quickly arranged my punishment—an entire month at a ranch in New Mexico, working with a friend of his from college.

I was surprised how fast Dad worked everything out. It was almost as if he'd been planning to ship me off across the country ever since we got the news about Mom. Like he just couldn't wait to get rid of me so he'd have one less thing to fix.

"It's for the best," he told me. "You know, with everything that's going on."

Dad's been using that phrase a lot lately. It was "for

the best" when he made me stop hanging out with Beto and Yesi in the library so I could do more chores at home. It was "for the best" when he said I had to quit the school anime club because my grades were slipping. It was "for the best" when he grounded me from playing video games after I called my PE teacher a wart-covered warlock.

Dad and I clearly have different definitions of *best*.

Stealing the slushie machine was apparently Dad's breaking point, after months of my grades slipping, calls from teachers, and whispered arguments so we wouldn't wake up Mom. Yesi swore in multiple languages that Dad was overreacting, since it was just one little prank. She promised to hide me under her bed for the month. Beto told me he'd come up with a cloaking spell to make me invisible all summer.

But I was on a plane to New Mexico before he could figure it out.

It was dark when Jonas Webber, the ranch director and Dad's friend from when they were both studying at the University of Miami, picked me up from the airport in Santa Fe and drove me to Rancho Espanto, my prison for the month. Rain pelted Jonas's Jeep our entire drive, so he said he'd show me around later. For all I knew, I'd landed in the stinky Hedor Swamps, my least favorite place in The Forgotten Age after Beto, Yesi, and I got stuck there on a quest when Yesi kept rolling a two.

Jonas informed me the ranch doesn't have cell service or internet, so I can't even text Beto and Yesi to complain about the ranch's poop smell. They made me promise to chat with them every day, but my only option here seems to be tying a note that says *Save me* to a bird's leg and launching it in the direction of Miami.

I sit up and rub my face. Stretching my back, I wonder if the mattress I slept on is stuffed with pine cones and rocks. After Jonas called Dad from the landline phone in his office to say I'd arrived safely, he showed me where I'd be staying—a small mud-colored building next to a long wooden fence. I thought maybe Dad had secretly sent me to one of those Scared Straight programs for at-risk youth. My room has a bed and a small dresser. The bathroom has the expected sink, toilet, and tiny shower but also a few surprise roommates, like the large spider perched on the shower faucet, waving its leg and daring me to bathe.

I skipped cleaning up last night.

I yank a shirt out of my suitcase and something floats to the floor. It's a photograph and a piece of paper. I pick up the photo and stare at me, Dad, and Mom standing in front of a Christmas tree. She must've snuck it in there when I was busy being yelled at by Dad. I touch the top of her head in the photo. She's about four inches taller than I am in the picture, and her long dark brown hair is flowing loose over her shoulders and down her arms.

She's an inch shorter than me now even though I haven't gone through any growth spurts. And her hair, well . . .

Grabbing the paper off the floor, I recognize Mom's careful handwriting.

¡Oye, Pollito! I can be sneaky just like your character, no?

I smile. Mom's been calling me Pollito since I was born. She said I was completely bald the first two years of my life and looked exactly like a plucked chicken. Thanks, Mom.

I know you don't want to be in New Mexico. Ño ñame, I wouldn't, either, honestly. How do people live so far away from the ocean? I couldn't stand it, ya tú sabes.

But before you know it, you'll be home soon. I'll try to make you a big plate of quesitos.

The last sentence of the letter is written so messily, I can barely read it. Mom must've gotten tired. But I think it says, *No hay mal que por bien no venga.*

I sigh, staring at Mom's handwriting. I don't understand how she can possibly believe that every cloud has a silver lining. Sometimes clouds are just a babosan bomb, dark and stormy, waiting to pelt you with rain or hail. And even after the clouds pass, your shoes are muddy and the air smells moldy.

Before Dad drove me to Miami International Airport, I hugged Mom, my arms wrapping completely around her, feeling each of her ribs. She went up on her toes to kiss me on the forehead. I wanted to cling to her as long as I could, but Dad, not looking me in the eye, grunted that we needed to go.

I set the photo on the dresser and tuck the letter under my pillow. As I change my clothes, I knock my shoes against the wall before I put them on, uncertain if Señor Spider found a new place to hang out and scare me.

Stepping outside, I glance around. Now that it's

light and the rain has stopped, I get a good look at my prison. The small building with my room is up on a hill, giving me a decent view of the rest of the ranch. There's only a few buildings here, tucked between towering rock cliffs that burn orange as the rising sun hits them. All of the buildings are exactly like mine— one story and covered with brown clay. Some of them have wooden poles sticking out under the roof, but I have no idea why. There's more dirt here than I've ever seen in my life, only broken up by scraggly bushes, rocks, and cacti. It's definitely like the Cambimuda Realm, where you have to battle shapeshifters that look different every time you come across them. Which is a way cooler place than the Hedor Swamps and probably where Beto, Yesi, and I would be adventuring all summer if I hadn't been exiled here.

I shove my hands in my pockets and groan as I stretch my neck. Even with the rain last night, the air is dry, and I cough.

Jonas explained that Rancho Espanto serves as an artists' retreat where painters come to be inspired by the landscapes. He told me a famous painter used to live in a cabin here. There's even a museum in Santa

Fe dedicated to her and filled with a collection of her huge flower paintings. So artists from all over the country come to Rancho Espanto because they want to be like her. They hike trails, ride horses, and take classes together. All I can think as I look around is they'd better be good at using every shade of brown in their paintings.

But Jonas also explained that the ranch is a place where scientists study. They work here digging up dinosaur bones, particularly of Coelophysis, the state dinosaur of New Mexico. I didn't know states had official dinosaurs.

And a ranch full of artists and scientists seems like an odd combination to me. I wonder what kind of job Jonas is going to give me to do. Refilling paint palettes for landscape painters? Digging in the dirt with paleon-tologists?

Ño, what if I get yelled at by a temperamental artist for not bringing them just the right shade of purple, and they zap me with a paintbrush because they're actually a wizard? What if one of the scientists is secretly an evil genius who's going to feed me to a reanimated veloci-raptor?

I breathe in the cool air. Dirt catches in my throat and I cough again.

Jonas told me to meet him at the administration building once I got up and he'd show me around. My stomach rumbles, and I hope part of Jonas's ranch tour will involve breakfast.

Heading around the back of my building, I find the source of the smell that so pleasantly woke me up this morning. A gray horse sticks his head over the long wooden fence and grunts at me, his breath sending little clouds out his nose. He paws the ground with his hoof and grunts again.

"You hungry for breakfast too, bro?" I ask, patting my stomach. "There's no chance they serve pastelitos or churros here, is there? Maybe a Publix sub sandwich?"

I start to reach out and rub the horse's snout, but I don't want to get my fingers bit off. Although, maybe a bloody stump for a hand would be a good reason to be sent home.

I glance past the horse and see a man in a dark green sweater that looks like it's been pecked apart by ravenous ostriches. He's mumbling to himself and kicking his worn shoes in the dirt as he strides along the fence.

I've always been afraid of strangers because the possibility that they're actually a halfling or an orc in disguise, waiting to kidnap and enslave me in their faraway country, is too high. But this guy, with his stringy dark brown hair falling over his face as his lips purse in a tight line, makes my stomach flop. He reaches the end of the fence line, and I inch closer to the horse next to me, deciding that a gnawed-off finger might be better than whatever this stranger might cook up.

The man looks up and stops in his tracks. His dark brown eyes bore into me, making me squirm. He kind of looks like my tío Benito, only thirteen times angrier. My hands start to tingle and I shake them at my side. The cool morning breeze picks up and whispers on the back of my neck, making me shiver.

The stranger down the fence line touches his thumb to each of his fingers as if he's counting over and over. I squeeze my hands in a tight fist when I realize I'm doing the same thing. It's something I always do when I'm nervous. Which is pretty much all the time.

But then the man raises his finger, points at me, and says in a scratchy voice, "You."

He turns on his heel, kicking up dirt, and runs back in the direction he came. I hear him mumbling over and over as he tears down the path.

"He's here."

CHAPTER 3

WHAT THE BABOSAN bomb was that?

I don't know how strong the fumes are in the paint the artists use here. But maybe this guy needs to work in a better-ventilated area. Mom would say he's one domino short of a full set. But she usually just says that to Dad when she's mad at him.

My body stopped shaking the second the man was out of sight, even though the brisk morning air is still kicking up dirt in my face.

Heading down a path, I pass buildings decorated with cow skulls complete with horns. They look like the masks rogues wear in The Forgotten Age. I think about taking a picture for Yesi but remember that not only do I not have a cell phone, it would be as good as a hunk of metal in this dirt-and-rock-covered prison. Even the Yermola Wasteland in The Forgotten Age has divining reeds to communicate with people in other realms.

Sending up swirls of dirt as I walk, I pass a few

buildings that look just like mine and I figure they also have rooms for people to stay in. They probably have Señor Spider's cousins for roommates, too. There's another larger building labeled DINING HALL and a building farther down the path from it with a sign that says RANCHO ESPANTO LIBRARY.

But that's it. If Rancho Espanto was part of The Forgotten Age, the world map would fit on a dusty sticky note surrounded by rocks.

I finally find a larger building labeled ADMINISTRATION, but Jonas is nowhere in sight. I sit on a bench on the porch and take in the cacti with small yellow flowers, the tall trees with waving branches, and the towering rock cliffs. And dirt. So much dirt.

It's already all over my pants and shoes, just from the walk here. I brush the calf of my pants as much as I can, leaving light orange streaks on my hands.

That's when I spot it. Crawling toward me, its spiny tail raised and ready to strike.

A scorpion.

Getting stung by that spiky danger noodle would be at least fifty damage points in The Forgotten Age.

Ño, this is how I die. Stung by a scorpion in Middle

of Nowhere, New Mexico, left to flail and froth at the mouth.

Not even Mom's Cuban cure-all chant, *Sana, sana, colita de rana*, can save me now.

Although it hasn't exactly done anything for her, either.

Just as quickly as I accept my certain death, a boot kicks the scorpion aside and it sails off the porch. It's probably disappointed that its plan to puncture my ankle was foiled.

I look up and see that the boot is attached to a girl about my age, with bright purple hair in two long braids hanging over her shoulders. She's wearing an oversized gray University of New Mexico hoodie and carrying two foil packets.

Before I can thank her, she takes a deep breath and says, "I read in a book that scorpions are related to spiders. Can you imagine going to that family reunion? Like, no thank you, please. The book also said that they can slow down their metabolisms so they can survive eating only one insect for a year. A whole entire year! Well, we can't do that, so here's some breakfast. Mr. Jonas told me to bring it to you."

"Th-thank you," I stammer, taking the foil packet she's holding out to me. I'm not sure if I'm thanking her for saving me from the scorpion, for giving me breakfast, or for the unwanted wealth of scorpion information she just dumped on me.

I unwrap the breakfast the girl handed me and poke my finger at what looks like a tortilla.

"It's a breakfast burrito," the girl explains. She unwraps hers and takes a large bite. Chewing with her mouth full, she says, "Well, not just any breakfast burrito, a Gearhart Special breakfast burrito."

"What's a Gearhart?"

"The Gearhart brothers. They're the cooks in our dining hall, and they make the best food ever. Like seriously so good. I bet you've never had food this amazing before."

I take a large bite of the burrito to test her theory. It's filled with warm and gooey eggs, beans, and cheese.

And something else.

My eyes water as my lips sting and my mouth burns. I bolt up from my seat on the bench, looking for a water fountain, a sink, a puddle of water . . . anything to cool my mouth.

"Ño!" I shriek.

Swallowing lava has to be at least eighty damage points.

"Huh, I didn't expect that," the girl says, looking at me. "I figured you'd be okay with spice. I mean, sure, the Gearhart brothers' food is usually melt-your-face-off spicy, but Jonas said your name was Rafael Alvarez. I thought you could handle it."

I don't even know where to begin with so many words, mostly because my throat has closed up. I start to cough.

The girl pulls something out of the pocket of her hoodie and holds it out to me.

It's a carton of milk. I open it quickly and guzzle, the burning in my throat slowly fading.

"I see you found the Gearhart brothers' famous green chili breakfast burritos," Jonas says as he walks up to us on the porch. He pats me on the back and I cough again, sending a white spray of milk toward the girl.

I nod, reminding myself to stick to the cereal whenever I'm in the dining hall at breakfast.

Jonas pushes his glasses up the bridge of his nose

and shakes his head. His sandy brown hair sticks out in all directions. "Your dad never liked spicy food, either. He used to get so mad at people who assumed he liked jalapeños and habañeros just because he was Cuban," he tells me.

I look directly at the girl. "Cuban food isn't spicy," I sputter, milk dribbling down my chin. It's weird to hear about my dad from his college days. To me, he's never been College Student Dad, only Realtor Dad, who wants to arrange his family to look perfect, just like he does houses.

The girl in front of me shrugs, shoving the last bite of her burrito in her mouth.

"Well, you already saw all of the ranch coming over here from the horse corral. So I figured it would be better to show you the scenery surrounding the ranch. That's why people come here!" Jonas says, clapping and smiling at the girl and me. "Ready to go? Let's head out."

I toss my empty carton of milk and uneaten lava burrito in a trash can next to the administration building and follow Jonas and the girl with the purple braids, a little overwhelmed by Jonas's enthusiasm for sightseeing dirt so early in the morning.

Jonas leads us to a trail that begins behind the administration building, the starting point marked by rough logs making a gateway, with another bleached cow skull at the top. For all I know, we're entering the Yermola Wasteland, and vicious blargmores will be crouched behind huge boulders, waiting to tattoo our kidneys for trespassing on their land.

I wonder what kind of person would choose to work here, especially after you've gone to college in Miami, with beaches, palm trees, and a lot less dirt. Like, way less dirt. Dad explained in grunts on the way to the airport that Jonas was an environmental science major who always wanted to be out in the middle of nowhere.

Wish granted, I guess.

As we continue up the trail, I realize I have bigger things to worry about than blargmores.

Because the trail is definitely up.

The dirt path keeps climbing and climbing as it meanders around cacti covered with long, sharp spines, and more rocks than I've ever seen in my life.

Miami is flat. So flat you never really get good momentum riding your skateboard. New Mexico is something else. The trail winds up and down, daring me to touch the thick white clouds hanging above.

"Okay, you've got to see this view," Jonas says, pausing on the trail and pointing out the valley below us. He's been stopping every so often to talk about the sights. I suspect he knows my lungs are about to explode and is giving me a break. "There's a dinosaur quarry down in the valley. The scientists that study here have found one of the world's largest collections of fossils. They even found the only complete fossil of a Coelophysis."

The girl with the purple braids comes up behind me. I notice she's not as out of breath as I am. "Did you know the whole ranch was won in a card game? Like, some really bad gambler bet all this in a game of poker. I'd make sure I was a pretty good player before I did something that stupid. But, like, then the guy's wife took it from him when they got divorced. As if this land should belong to anyone other than the native people that first lived here," she explains.

I nod and put my hands on my hips, trying to catch my breath without making it obvious to Jonas and the girl that I'm dying. Physical activity isn't exactly my favorite pastime. I'd been taking slow walks with Mom up and down the sidewalk in front of our house, but those had gotten shorter and shorter lately. I wonder if Dad is making sure she still goes outside.

I shake my head and suck in warm air as the girl holds out a water bottle to me.

"You should keep drinking. The dry air makes you dehydrate quickly. Like, shrivel up like a raisin nobody's gonna want to eat. Because, I mean, who really likes raisins anyways? And sorry about that burrito. Didn't mean to shove a fire grenade down your throat your first day here. Not much of a welcome wagon, I guess. But, like, what did you say after you ate it? Was it a Spanish curse word? Because I've always wanted to be a multilingual curser."

"Thanks," I tell her. "And I said *ño*."

"No?"

"Ño. Say it like there's a *y* shoved in there. Nyo. It's pretty much an all-purpose Cuban word. Are you excited? Say ño. Scared? Ño. Angry?"

"Ño!" the girl interjects. "So if I don't speak a lick of Spanish, I can just say ño all the time and I'll be fine? That's awesome. I now officially speak three languages. Mom's gonna be so proud of me."

I realize I have no idea what her name is, and in the

breathless monologues she's given me, she's never said.

"So I guess you know that I'm Rafa Alvarez and I can't handle spicy food. Who are you?" I ask.

The girl flips a braid over her shoulder as Jonas leads us farther up the trail.

"Oh, oops. I'm Jennie Kim. My mom is the librarian here at the ranch. I mostly work there all day, but Mr. Jonas said there was finally going to be another kid on the ranch and I should come on this hike with you so you'd feel welcome. There's never any kids here. Just super-serious scientists and super-serious artists."

"I saw there was a library here. That's pretty cool, I guess. For a place like this, I mean." We've started hiking, and I'm breathing hard again.

Jonas keeps charging up the trail, his feet kicking up dirt behind him and into my face. I cough. For someone who drives like an eighty-year-old grandma, as I learned when he picked me up from the airport, Jonas attacks the trail like he's being chased by a pack of rabid blargmores.

Jennie nods enthusiastically and then looks me up and down, taking in my heaving chest struggling for breath and my cheeks, which I'm certain are blazing red.

"Hey, Mr. Jonas," she calls up ahead. "Look at that. Isn't that, like, the most beautiful thing you've ever seen in your entire life? Like, paint it and hang it over your couch, right?"

Jennie stops and points to the valley in front of us. A massive reddish brown cliff towers on the other side. I've never seen anything so tall. We've been hiking past the same rock face for an hour, but it seems like it keeps morphing and changing color as the sun climbs in the sky and different clouds sail overhead. We've got a bird's-eye view of the entire ranch, the low buildings tucked in between the cliffs. Off in the distance, I spot rocks laid out in a circle, with a pattern inside like a maze. It looks like one of the official seals of The Forgotten Age.

"That's pretty cool," I say to Jennie.

Jonas comes up next to me. "High praise. Your dad wasn't a big fan of hiking, either. One spring break, I convinced him to do part of the Appalachian Trail with me. We barely made it five miles. But at least I learned every single Spanish curse word."

I smirk, thinking about Dad suffering the same fate at the hands of Jonas as I am now. And I've been saying all the Spanish curse words in my head, too.

Mom was always the more adventurous one in our family anyways, dragging me out to the Everglades or down to the Keys so she could sketch flowers and plants for her sculptures. We haven't gone on a trip like that for a year.

I take a deep breath, hoping Jonas and Jennie will let me rest a little longer. "So, um, I have a question for you two," I tell them, brushing dirt off my pants.

"Shoot," Jonas says.

"So let's say you're walking in the forest one day and you come across a wild alimancita—"

"What's an alimancita?" Jennie asks.

"It's a hamster-lizard hybrid from The Forgotten Age, this role-playing game I play with my friends Beto and Yesi."

Jonas moves like he's going to keep storming up the trail, but I stand firm, hoping he'll stay with Jennie and me and enjoy the valley view.

"So there's this wild alimancita stuck high up in this tree," I continue. "What would you do in that situation?"

Jennie smiles, playing with the end of her braid. She flips it over her shoulder and says, "Oh my gosh. That sounds amazing. I know exactly what I would do. I mean, I'm probably some fantastic warrior wizard princess in this place, right? Yeah, that's definitely what I am. So I would have no problem using my magic wand made out of the bones of my enemies to get the alimancita thing down."

I snort on the gulp of water I took from my water bottle and it shoots out my nose.

Jonas smirks. "You're giving us a 'save the cat' situation to figure out what kind of people we are, aren't you?"

"Maybe," I say, even though I'm completely busted. Beto, Yesi, and I always ask this question from The Forgotten Age to learn about people we meet. It's used to develop your player character in the game. Beto's character convinces a child to save the alimancita and ends up injuring both in the process. I sit and watch until the alimancita figures out how to get down from the tree on its own.

Yesi sets the tree on fire.

Jonas raises his arms above his head and stretches. "Well, I suppose I'd avoid the evil wizard, rescue the hamster-creature thing, and make sure the tree wasn't damaged when I did it. Cover all my bases, you know? And no grinding of my enemies' bones necessary."

"You're no fun, Mr. Jonas," Jennie says, winking.

When I'd asked Dad the question, he just said it was stupid and went back to typing on his laptop. Mom said she'd create a world where the alimancita wouldn't have gotten caught in the tree in the first place.

I can understand why she'd want to change the past.

Jonas turns and scampers up the trail again, like a kindergartner trying to make it to the bathroom in time. Jennie and I have no choice but to follow him.

"Did you know cattle rustlers used to hide cows in the valley here?" Jennie asks, walking next to me even though I'm certain she could run up the trail just like Jonas.

"Cattle rustlers?" I ask.

"Guys who steal cows. There were these two brothers who were super notorious in, like, the early 1900s for stealing cattle and hiding them between the cliffs. They even spread rumors that the area was haunted by ghosts to keep people away. They strung up dummies in trees to make people think there were monsters everywhere. That's how the ranch got its name, Rancho Espanto," Jennie tells me.

"I wondered about that. I thought it was a joke," I say. "I mean, Terror Ranch? Not gonna attract a lot of visitors with that one."

Jennie laughs, her high pitch echoing off the canyon walls.

"So . . . what happened . . . to those cattle rustler bros? They get caught?" My lungs burn again and I wonder if Jennie is strong enough to carry me the rest of the way on the trail.

"Oh, the Arnoldson brothers? It's a pretty creepy story, really. But, like, those are the best stories. Travelers who came through the area looking for a place to rest would stay with the brothers and then disappear, all their possessions magically ending up with the Arnoldsons. I think they pushed the travelers off cliffs or drowned them in their well. At night, if you listen really closely, you can still hear their victims screaming in the wind."

"Ño."

"Jennie, quit trying to scare Rafa," Jonas calls over his shoulder as he barrels up the trail.

"I'm just stating facts, Mr. Jonas," Jennie replies, dismissing him with a wave of her hand. "Eventually the brothers got in this huge argument with each other over some gold they had stolen, and one of them ended up killing the other. Right after that happened, the people in the area found the surviving Arnoldson brother and hung him from a tree."

Jonas, Jennie, and I round a corner on the trail and my feet slide in the dirt, pulling me toward the edge of the cliff. My heart jumps in my throat and I catch my balance. Looking out over the rocks, I spot movement down in the valley below us. I squint and see three brown-and-white cows, their hooves scraping the rocks as they nod their horns side to side. They scamper together as if being rounded up by some invisible cowboy, their snorts echoing off the canyon walls.

"Are there still people who keep cows in the canyon?" I ask Jennie.

"What? No, the land is protected. You can't use it for any kind of farming or ranching," she responds.

I look again at the cows, their eyes wide as they push one another against the rocks.

"Really? What about those cows down there?" I point below us into the canyon.

Jennie trots over next to me and looks down. "What cows?"

I look again and see an empty valley, the wind whipping between the rocks. I scan up and down the ravine, but it's empty. No cows in sight.

Jennie smacks me on the back and I jump. "Let's keep going, Rafa. I think you might be a little dehydrated."

I shake my head, still certain of what I saw on the rocks as the wind howls in my ears.

CHAPTER 4

I CAN'T FEEL my legs. The moment I wake up, I reach for my twenty-sided die on the nightstand next to my bed and tell it: "I am never going to walk again and will have to crawl on my elbows and knees for the rest of my life."

I flip it on the mattress next to me and the number nineteen faces up at me and laughs.

Mom would tell me "Ño ñaque!" and go on about how amazing it was that I had tried something new and hiked so far. She likes to add other words that start with *ñ* to the typical Cuban phrase because there aren't a lot of them and they make silly, nonsense sayings. But that's just how she is.

And my aching muscles would cry at her enthusiasm. I mean, how enthusiastic she used to be. Before . . .

I groan and get out of bed. Jonas told me I had to

report to the horse stables behind my building at eight. I slept late, practically a corpse after his death march with Jennie yesterday. And even as tired as I was, I couldn't get the thought of the disappearing cows out of my head. Between ghost bovine, muttering strangers who seem freaked out by me, and Jennie's stories of outlaw brothers, I wonder what in the babosan bomb kind of place Dad has exiled me to.

I've got just enough time to run to the dining hall, grab breakfast, and get back to the barn. I dress quickly, gasping each time I move as my muscles scream at me. I stuff on my shoes after I turn them over. Jonas advised me to always store them upside down so spiders and scorpions wouldn't make my stinky shoes their new home.

Jogging to the dining hall, my legs protest, and I have to stop and catch my breath before I collapse in the dirt. Once I finally get there, I quickly grab bread and make myself a peanut butter and honey sandwich, ignoring the scrambled eggs the Gearhart brothers keep trying to give me because I spot a mountain of not-so-stealthy green chilies peeking out from the runny yolks.

You're not getting me today, bro.

Scarfing down my sandwich, I power walk back to the barn, my legs still yelling at me not to run. I pass four horses standing inside a wooden fence. They snort and scratch their hooves in the dirt. Entering the long barn past the horses, I see a row of small open rooms on either side of an aisle. I'm not sure who I'm supposed to meet or what I'm supposed to be doing. I stand there, staring at the horses as they ignore me. Their tails flick as flies land on their backs.

I look down at the end of the barn toward a large open door that overlooks a gate. The man from my first morning on the ranch is standing there, toying with a link of chains that holds the gate closed. He turns and gasps when he sees me. Dropping the chains from the gate, he points to me again, his long, bony finger shaking.

"You. You can't be here. You need to leave," he says, his eyes darting around the barn.

"Why?" I yell out to him, the horses in the barn huffing and kicking from the sudden noise. The man takes three hurried steps toward me, his feet shuffling in the dirt. He opens his mouth to say something, but his eyes grow wide when he looks past me. Before I can ask him anything else, he turns and runs away from the barn.

"You here to work?" a gruff voice asks behind me.

I whip around and face the largest man I've ever seen in my life. He looks like he could be a formidable Forgotten Age warrior, and I'm pretty sure his forearm is as big as my thigh. His curly black hair is shaved close to his head at the sides and a little bit longer at the top. But nowhere near as long as my hair, which I flip off my forehead.

"Um, yeah," I stammer, nervous under the man's hard eyes. "Did you, uh, see that guy in the green sweater?"

"A guy?" the man asks, his black eyebrow arching.

"Yeah, in a green sweater."

"A green sweater?"

I know better than to roll my eyes, because this man looks like he could flick my intestines straight out of my belly button in a snap.

The stern expression on the man's face breaks and he smirks. "I'm just messing with you, man. Ain't nobody else here. Nobody likes the smell of horse manure. Keeps folks away, just like I like it."

I nod and shove my hands in the pockets of my jeans.

"You drink coffee?" the man asks.

"Yes?" If you consider the café con leche from the ventanita near my house that has more milk than actual coffee. And a whole lot of sugar. I used to run there before school to get Mom a colada and pastelito before her stomach decided it didn't like acidic food anymore. I wonder if Dad is making sure she eats the mashed banana and toast that's become her regular breakfast.

"Good. Come with me," he says, walking down the middle of the barn and stopping inside a small office. His massive height and broad shoulders fill up the room, so I stand outside, leaning on the doorframe.

"What's your name, little man?" he asks as he pulls two narrow red packets out of a desk in the office. He rips them open with his teeth and dumps them into two mugs. I notice a massive tattoo on his bicep, almost blending into his dark brown skin. It looks like a parachute with wings sprouting from each side that wrap around his arm.

Beto's brother, Guillermo, has a tattoo of a rifle

with leaves that wrap around it. He says it's his combat infantry tattoo. I would always stare at it whenever Guillermo drove me to the hospital because the barrel of the rifle seemed to point at his head.

Distracted, I realize I haven't answered the man's question. "Rafael Alvarez," I say.

Pouring hot water from an electric kettle into the mugs and stirring them, the man says, "Alvarez. Sounds good." Guillermo always wants to call me by my last name, too.

"I actually go by Rafa."

"Alvarez it is." The man hands me a mug. "I'm Marcus Coleman."

"Marcus it is," I say, taking the mug and raising my eyebrows.

The man smirks and dumps a spoonful of white powder in my mug and does the same to his own. He swirls the mug around and swigs the coffee down in one massive gulp.

I sniff the coffee and take a sip. A spoiled, acidic taste washes over my tongue and I try not to gag. I figure I'd better use Marcus's method and I swallow down the mug of coffee as quickly as I can without scalding my throat. The rancid flavor makes me gag, and I can't hide my pursed lips and squinting eyes.

I'm sure I've just suffered twenty damage points for drinking poisoned coffee.

Marcus chuckles. "I know. It's not great. But you drink the same thing for eight years, you get used to it. No matter how bad."

I hand my mug back to Marcus. "Why would you drink something like this . . . for eight years?"

"Afghanistan doesn't have Starbucks." Marcus flicks his thumb on the rim of the coffee cup and looks at me, his eyes taking in every pimple on my chin and the strands of hair glued with nervous sweat to my forehead.

I nod and give a half smile, unsure what to say. "Um, so can I ask you something?"

"I don't know anything about no man in a green sweater," Marcus says, smirking.

I shake my head. "No, not that. I was wondering what you would do if you were walking in the forest one day and you came across an alimancita trapped in a tree by an evil wizard. It's a lizard-hamster kind of thing."

"The wizard?"

"No, the alimancita."

"That coffee didn't sit well with you, did it?" Marcus winks at me. He takes a deep breath. "Well, why wouldn't I just climb the tree and get it down?"

"It's like a hundred feet in the air, practically no branches to hang on to, the wind is blowing a million miles an hour and could pummel you to the ground any second."

Marcus looks me square in the eye. "Still not a problem. I'd climb the tree."

He rolls his shoulders and his shirt stretches across his chest. I'm surprised he didn't say he'd rip the tree out of the ground by its roots.

"My turn," Marcus says, crossing his arms. "Why'd you get sent here? Webber says you're from Miami. What's a Florida kid doing by himself in New Mexico?"

I scuff my foot on the floor and shove my hands in my pockets. "There's a chance I tried to steal the slushie machine from my school cafeteria."

"How big a chance?"

"One hundred percent."

Marcus raises an eyebrow. "So is this your punishment or something?"

I nod. "Yeah. My dad and Mr. Webber know each other because they went to college together. They arranged the whole thing when my dad decided to completely overreact. He just wants me out of the way since my mom—"

I stop myself as the coffee churns in my stomach, threatening to make a second appearance all over the floor of Marcus's office. I don't know why I'm telling Marcus so much.

Marcus takes a clipboard off a nail in the wall and scans the papers on it. "Well, I wouldn't beat yourself up about it too much. There's a chance I once bought a goat from a local market and hid it in my captain's room. It ate two of his uniforms."

"How big a chance?"

"One hundred percent," Marcus says, winking.

"My friend Beto's brother was in Afghanistan, too. Guillermo was a combat infantryman. I think that's what it's called. He told me one time he used a Humvee to push over a Porta Potty with someone in it."

Marcus chuckles, his deep voice filling the small

office. Tossing the clipboard on his desk, he claps. "You ready to get to work?"

I'd rather drink more of Marcus's coffee, honestly.

I quickly realize that working with Marcus means I have to learn an entirely new vocabulary. And, trust me, English was one of my lowest grades last year. Mom always used to help me, making sure I looked up words I didn't know and helping me find books I'd like to read.

But she doesn't have the energy for that anymore.

"You need to give a flake of hay to Frankie, Wattson, Mia, and Jiji in their stalls," Marcus tells me before going off to get some other horses ready for a trail ride a group of artists are taking so they can paint landscapes farther into the canyon.

My first vocabulary lesson was that stalls are what they call the little rooms the horses stay in. Marcus stifled a chuckle when I asked him about that.

Alone in the barn, I find the hay stored in one of the stalls where Marcus told me it would be. Unfortunately, he didn't explain how much a "flake" is. Like a flake of dandruff?

Whatever it is, a flake feels like a tiny amount. I pinch a few sprigs of hay between my fingers and walk down the stalls looking for the right horses. I pass small plaques labeled TEXAS TRUE BLUE, MY JUAN LIGHT, CARA ME AWAY, and JAHAMA GHAZI.

I'm wondering who in the babosan bomb named these horses . . . and if dry air–induced dehydration drove them mad.

But I don't see any plaques for Frankie, Wattson, Mia, or Jiji. I see one for a horse named Ike, but Marcus didn't tell me to feed him. I have no idea who I'm supposed to give my handful of hay to.

I stand in the middle of the barn, sprigs of hay between my fingers in each hand. I get dizzy spinning in a circle scanning up and down the stalls for the right horses.

I'm going to get fired; I just know it. If I rolled my die and asked it if I was going to get booted on my first day working, it would land right on twenty and laugh. Ño, they're going to march me through the middle of the ranch, past all the scientists, artists, and workers so they can throw green chilies at me and shout, "This city boy doesn't know anything!"

I hear a throat clear behind me.

"Whatcha doing there, Alvarez?"

I lower my arms in defeat. "Honestly? I have absolutely no idea."

Marcus chuckles. "Well, that much is clear. What's that in your hands?"

I open my palms and a breeze blows the few bits of hay I had onto the floor of the barn. "A flake of hay?"

A low laugh erupts from Marcus's throat and he doubles over, hands across his stomach. His voice echoes in the barn and the horse behind me snorts.

He's laughing at me, too.

"All right. I should've explained this. I'm not used to working with someone else here." Marcus walks over to the stall with the hay and scoops a massive pile between his arms. "This is how much a flake is, more or less."

I nod, just as the horse in the stall next to us snorts at my ignorance and kicks the wooden wall with his hoof. The sharp smack echoes through the barn, and I jump.

I look at Marcus, waiting for him to explain where the correct horses are, but his lips are in a tight line and his eyes are squeezed shut. His chest heaves as hay starts to fall from his arms.

I'm not sure what to do so I just stand there. A fly lands on the back of my hand and I wave it off.

Finally, Marcus takes a deep breath and bends over, picking up a flake of hay again. He nods for me to do the same, as if nothing has happened.

Walking down the barn aisle, Marcus stops in front of a stall with a plaque labeled CARA ME AWAY. "Let's feed Mia first," he tells me.

"But that doesn't say this is Mia," I respond, raising my eyebrow.

I feel like I'm on a quest in The Forgotten Age, searching for morphling horses in the Cambimuda Realm with a fierce warrior as my guide. But I don't tell Marcus that.

He shakes his head, lifting the stall latch with his elbow and shoving the flake of hay in a feeder by the door. "Oh, right. Forgot to tell you about that, too."

I wonder about all the other things Marcus might have forgotten to tell me.

He motions for me to dump my hay in the feeder as well. "Okay, so here's the deal. Horses tend to have two names. Their registered name, in this case Cara Me Away, and their barn name, Mia."

He walks me down the barn aisle and shows me that Texas True Blue is also Frankie, My Juan Light is Wattson, and Jahama Ghazi is Jiji. I repeat the names in my head to try to remember.

The horse next to the hay stall, Frankie, kicks his hoof against the wall again. It's not as loud as before, since we're not directly next to it, but I notice Marcus tense up and clench his fists.

Frankie kicks the stall again and Marcus's eyes go wide. He pushes past me hard, accidentally shoving me to the ground. The barn floor is cold and rough against my hands as I watch Marcus stomp over to Frankie's stall and punch his fist against the wooden door. I cower as Marcus seethes, narrowing his eyes at Frankie.

"Stow it!" he shouts, spit flying from his mouth as he lets loose a string of curses that would have Mom flinging a chancla at my head in one second flat.

I scoot away from him and stand up, brushing hay from my jeans.

I watch as Marcus takes a deep breath and rests his head against the door of the stall, his fists still clenched as his chest heaves.

"I think you'd better call it a day, Alvarez," he says without looking at me.

"Okay," I mumble, hurrying down the barn aisle. I leave through the large doors at the back of the barn and spot the chain link for the horse pasture's gate hanging loose and clanking against the metal bars. The sound echoes in my ears as I put more distance between my scurrying footsteps and Marcus's fists pounding the wall in the barn.

CHAPTER 5

LAST SEPTEMBER, I was having dinner at Beto's house. Mom was too tired to cook and Dad was on some business trip to Orlando. Beto's brother, Guillermo, had been home from Afghanistan for two months. In the middle of us eating picadillo and frijoles negros and joking about our latest escapade in The Forgotten Age, Guillermo slammed his fist on the table, knocking over Beto's water glass.

"Quiet!" he'd screamed, before storming off to his room.

Beto and I never figured out what set Guillermo off. But after that, he met with a therapist every week and that really seemed to help.

I wonder who's here to help Marcus.

Heading away from the barn, I realize it's not even time for lunch and I'm already done with work for the day. Unsure of what to do with myself, I trudge over to the library Jennie told me about.

A woman smiles when I enter and says, "Annyeong-haseyo! You must be Rafa!"

"Um . . . hola?"

The woman chuckles. She looks exactly like Jennie except she has long black hair instead of purple. And her mouth doesn't twist in a mischievous grin. "I'm Lisa Kim, Jennie's mom and the librarian here. My abuji always said it's good to learn one new word a day. So I'm teaching you how to say hello in Korean."

I shake my head. "Thanks, but no thanks. I learned enough new words this morning to make your abuji happy for a solid month. And what's an abuji?"

"Father."

"See? You taught me two words. You don't have to teach me one tomorrow. Assuming I'm here tomorrow and my brain hasn't exploded."

"That bad, huh?" Ms. Kim flips her hair over her shoulder and I spot two letters, RK, tattooed inside a heart on her wrist.

"Yeah. I learned that if you call stalls 'little horse rooms,' certain people will think you're maybe not so smart. And a flake of hay is way more than it sounds

54

like. And horses must be secret agents because they all have two names."

I look at Ms. Kim and she's biting her lip, trying not to laugh. "You'll get used to it," she says. "I bet you're a fast learner."

I wonder if I should tell her about what just happened with Marcus. But it doesn't seem like my business to say.

"Well, feel free to look around. This library is amazing, but I may be biased. It's a private library for the ranch so the artists and scientists who come here have everything they need to do their work. We've got lots of stories and information! Oh, and there's a chance we have the most desirable thing on the entire ranch," Ms. Kim says, winking.

"What's that?"

"Internet. You can email your family or your friends on the computer in my office any time you want. Just let me know."

My stomach flips. I think about emailing Beto and Yesi and telling them all about traversing the Yermola Wasteland and seeing ghost cows. About how the barn is as stinky as the Hedor Swamps. About the fire burritos served in the dining hall. About the weird guy in the green sweater who keeps yelling at me for no reason.

I think about emailing Mom.

But I don't know what I'd say.

Ms. Kim walks over to a cart piled with books and picks up several in her arms. I scan the spines on the cart and see one that says *Alexander Calder: A Life in Art*.

"Can I borrow this?" I ask, holding the book up.

Ms. Kim looks at the cover. "Of course! Do you like sculptures?"

I nod. "My mom is actually a metal sculpture artist. Or, like, she was. Calder is one of her favorite artists."

Rubbing my thumb along the spine, I think of the twisting bronze birds Mom created in her workroom, soaring up to the ceiling. It's my favorite sculpture she's made. Right after she finished it, she got a call from her doctor. There weren't many sculptures after that, but I always liked to stare at the birds reaching up to the ceiling of her workroom.

I take a deep breath, shoving the memory to the back of my mind. Spotting another book on the cart,

The History of Northeastern New Mexico, I figure it might have information about the creepy Arnoldson brothers that Jennie told me about, so I grab it and tuck it under my arm.

Thanking Ms. Kim, I wander to the back of the small library and meander along the shelves. I scan the spines of the books, not really looking for anything in particular. The book titles start to swirl and blend together. I reach for a red book and flip through the pages.

Multiple myeloma is a blood disorder . . .

A lump starts to grow in my throat and I swallow hard.

Patients commonly experience osteoporosis and bone degradation, which can affect height and structure . . .

Heat rises to my cheeks as tears pool in the corners of my eyes.

Under chemotherapy treatment, patients often lose their hair and suffer nausea as well as a lack of energy . . .

"What are you reading?" a voice says next to me.

I slam the book shut and return it to the shelf. I turn

and face Jennie. She's still wearing an oversized University of New Mexico hoodie, but this time it's cherry colored.

"You wanna be a doctor or something?" she asks as she twirls her braids between her fingers.

"No. I was just browsing," I say.

She looks me up and down. "This is the boring book section. I'll show you where the better books are."

She grabs my hand and, before I can react, drags me to a small room in the library, her bright purple hair swinging behind her. Standing in front of a shelf, she points and says, "This is the best section in the whole library. In any library. Probably in the whole world."

"Okay," I manage to croak out, and I watch Jennie twirl her braid again as she scans the book spines with her finger. "Why is this the best section?"

"Oh my gosh, obviously because it's the graphic novel section. They're only the most amazing books in the entire universe. And all the other universes we haven't discovered yet."

I smile. Jennie isn't wrong, even though she may be just a bit overenthusiastic in her opinion.

I browse the books and find a favorite. "Have you read this one?"

I show her a book with a cover of a boy, in a blue hoodie and backpack, staring at a piece of paper.

The girl's eyes grow big. "Are you kidding me? It's amazing. Definitely in my top five."

She bounces on her toes and pulls a book from the shelf. "Have you read this one? It's about the Constitution. Like, are you kidding me? A graphic novel about the Constitution. It's so cool."

She shoves the book in my hands and pulls another from the shelf. "And this one. It's about the Donner Party. Oh my gosh, a graphic novel about people eating one another. Seriously awesome."

I bite my lip to stifle a laugh as the book is pushed into my arms along with another about the history of poison and another about war photographers.

"So you like nonfiction?" I ask.

Jennie's chest heaves as she takes a deep breath. I think it's the first time I've seen her breathe since we started our conversation. I'm slightly certain the only other kid in all of Rancho Espanto is a small but fearsome Forgotten Age winsel in real life, known for their ability to overload any traveler they meet with a mountain of facts.

"Nonfiction, fiction, graphic novels, comics, web-toons, encyclopedias, fan fiction, audiobooks, subtitles in movies. I like them all. I like stories. I like information."

She grabs my hand again and drags me to a new bookcase. I have to balance the books she's given me so I don't drop them.

"But I especially like this," she says, pointing to a new shelf.

"Picture books? Aren't we a little old for those?"

Jennie rolls her eyes. "Okay, first of all, you're never too old for picture books. That's just a ridiculous thought right there. But the best part of this particular section of the library is this."

She removes five books next to one another and reaches behind them on the shelf, extracting a medium-sized, shiny maroon bag. Putting the books back, she holds the bag out to me.

"This is the part of the library where I hide my snacks," she says, winking.

I smile as my stomach rumbles.

We sit in two chairs in the library as she opens the bag.

"Are we allowed to eat in here?" I ask as I set the books she's given me on a low table in front of us.

"Yes?" Jennie answers, raising an eyebrow. I don't quite believe her but take the spiral-shaped chip she's holding out to me anyway. It's crunchy, sweet, and just a little bit sticky.

"These are honey twists," she explains as she hands me another chip, and I gobble it down. "They're the best snack in the whole world. Mom and I drive to the Korean market in Albuquerque and buy up whole bags of them."

I nod as she holds the bag out to me, and I grab a handful.

"So did you work with Mr. Marcus this morning?"

"Yeah," I tell her. "But, uh, we got done with all our chores pretty quick."

Jennie shoves a handful of honey twists in her mouth. "Oh my gosh, Mr. Marcus is like the coolest person on the planet. Did you know he was in the army? He used to jump out of airplanes. Like, perfectly good airplanes! Just jumped right out of them."

"I definitely would never jump out of a plane," I tell Jennie. "What if your parachute got holes eaten in it by moths? What if a helicopter flies too close to you and chops you into bits? I don't like flying in planes even when the doors are closed. Ño. No way I'd fly in them if the entire back was open, waiting to suck me out."

Jennie slaps her knee and laughs. "I think I might skydive someday. It sounds fun. Did you know the first woman paratrooper here in the United States was Bennis Blue? She did it way back in 1978. I bet she was totally awesome."

I scrunch my eyebrows as I take more honey twists, the crumbs sticking to my fingers. "How do you even know that?"

Jennie shrugs. "My dad was a history professor at the University of New Mexico. He used to give me all sorts of cool history facts."

I wonder why she used past tense. "Does he not teach there anymore?"

Jennie shakes her head and says, "No. He died two years ago."

I swallow the partially chewed honey twist in my

mouth and it scratches down my throat. My mind flashes to the heart tattoo on Ms. Kim's wrist. I start to say something, but my brain is empty.

Jennie waves her hand at me, dismissing my lack of a reaction. She points to the book at the bottom of my stack, *The History of Northeastern New Mexico.*

"If you really want to find out about the area, like the really good and important information, I have the perfect book for you."

Before I can respond, Jennie bolts up from her chair and runs to another section in the library. She returns with a small brown book in her hand.

As she sets it on the table in front of us, I read the title written in stamped silver letters.

Ghosts of Haunted New Mexico.

We flip through the book together, reading about a ghoul-filled abandoned hospital, a child ghost in a theater who has to be bribed with donuts, and a hotel where practically every guest mysteriously vanished. No mention of two brothers murdering travelers and stealing cattle, though.

No mention of a man in a green sweater wandering around a ranch and yelling at people, either.

We sit in silence, engrossed in our books. Every once in a while, Jennie points out an old, faded photograph or reads a particularly spooky paragraph out loud. I do the same. It's what Beto, Yesi, and I would always do at the library in Miami.

Before I had to stay home more to help Mom.

But this feels nice. Listening to Jennie and me flip pages, munch on honey twists, and let ourselves gasp at the tiniest things in the book drowns out the sound in my mind of Marcus's fist against the barn stall, the strange man's shouts, and Mom's whimpers at night.

CHAPTER 6

COLD AIR SWIRLS around me, tucking under my shirt and creeping up my spine. I shiver as the rocks in my shoes dig into my heels. Scrambling up the dirt path along the cliff, I look down and see a herd of cows scraping their hooves on the sun-bleached boulders.

One large brown cow looks at me, its eyes glowing red.

I run fast, dust kicking up behind me, and hear shouts chasing after me.

"What are you doing here? Go away!" a gruff voice yells, the sound bouncing off the rocks and multiplying until it morphs into an angry chorus.

I run faster, my lungs stinging as I cough on the dirt in the air. I cast a glance over my shoulder and see a green blur charging up the trail behind me.

"Why? Why did you do it?" the man in the worn green sweater screams at me.

I try to run faster, but the rocks in my shoes grow bigger and cut into the bottom of my feet. I look up ahead on the path as boulders tumble down the cliff face towering over me. They bounce down the path, cracks echoing in the air as they careen into one another. The noise grows louder as the boulders careen down the path right at me.

Just as a large rock heads straight for my face, my eyes slam open and I wake up, the morning light streaming through my window.

But the pounding doesn't stop.

I realize someone is knocking on my cabin door. I scramble out of bed, my blanket twisted around my legs, and stumble across the floor. Opening the door, I see Marcus.

"We gotta go, Alvarez. Horses got out and you need to help me round them up. They could trample a dig site or get lost in the canyon." Marcus nods at me and coughs. "Meet me at the barn. Preferably wearing pants."

I look down and see that I'm still wearing my bright yellow SpongeBob pajamas.

Trying to shake off my dream, I barely process what

he's telling me. Closing the door, I quickly change and then run to the barn.

"Follow me," Marcus says when he sees me. I walk next to him, straining to keep up with his long stride, as we head behind the barn to where a four-wheeler is parked, with Jennie standing next to it.

"Oh my gosh, Rafa, we get to ride in Mr. Marcus's side-by-side," she says, entirely too enthusiastic for how early it is. "This is going to be the best day ever. I know it. We get to save the horses before they get eaten by Vivarón, the thirty-foot-long snake that protects this land."

"That's just a story, Kim, and you know it," Marcus says.

Jennie twists a braid between her fingers and winks at me. "Is it, though? Are you sure?"

"You ever ridden one of these things?" Marcus asks, ignoring Jennie's comment. I start to scan the rocks around us for snakes.

I shake my head. "No, my mom wouldn't let me."

Yesi's cousin had a bunch of four-wheelers at their house in Homestead that they used to run around the edge of the Everglades. Mom told me if she ever caught me on one, she'd cook my fingers into her arroz con pollo.

She probably wouldn't notice if I rode one these days.

"Well, hop on," Marcus says, gesturing next to himself as he slides behind the wheel of the side-by-side. Jennie sits in the seat behind me, her legs bouncing up and down with excitement, shaking the entire vehicle.

We ride in silence, the only sound the side-by-side's tires spinning in the dirt, and I wonder what exactly is involved in getting loose horses back. I wait for Marcus to explain it to me, but when I look at him, he's chewing on his bottom lip and staring straight ahead.

Finally, he takes a deep breath. "Listen, Alvarez," he says. "About yesterday—"

"Have you ever had goat poop coffee?" I ask, interrupting him.

"What?" Marcus raises his eyebrows at me as we continue across the ridge. The side-by-side bounces on the rocks and I grab the edge of my seat.

"Yeah, so there's this kind of coffee where the beans

are eaten by goats and then they poop them out and people make coffee from the poop beans."

Jennie slaps me on the shoulder and says, "That sounds awesome. I mean, how many people can say they've had goat poop coffee? I bet it tastes like recycled grass and amazingness."

Marcus shakes his head. "Why are you telling me this?"

I shrug. "I was just thinking that it probably tastes better than your coffee."

Marcus tries to swallow a chuckle, but it escapes from his mouth and bounces off the windshield in front of us.

He doesn't have to explain anything about yesterday to me. Sometimes things just happen. Sometimes you roll a two and can't get out of the dark dungeon no matter how much you want to. Sometimes you come upon a devious blargmore who tricks you into giving away all your treasure. Sometimes your mom has to spend a month in the hospital and you're not allowed to visit her so you call your PE teacher a wart-covered warlock the next day.

Sometimes things just happen.

"So, is it gonna be hard to get these horses back?" I ask. What I really want to ask is what are my odds of being trampled to death in an angry horse stampede? What are the chances I'll be thrown into a pile of prickly cacti, their spines impaling my eyeballs?

"Naw. They're big, dumb animals. But you still need to be careful. Dumb things can be dangerous," Marcus explains.

I'm going to end up with a horseshoe imprint on my forehead, I know it.

Marcus gestures down into a valley beyond the ridge. "There they are."

I look over the rocks and spot five horses standing aimlessly, munching on grass and scratching their hooves in the dirt. Thankfully, there isn't a thirty-foot-long snake anywhere in sight.

Marcus slowly maneuvers the side-by-side across the rocks and down the ridge. I grab on to my seat so tightly I think my bones might burst through my knuckles. I'm going to die in some freak four-wheeler accident and Mom is going to write TE LO DIJE on my gravestone, announcing to the world that she told me so.

Marcus positions the side-by-side behind the horses. One gives us a lazy glance and goes back to chomping on a scraggly plant growing out from under a rock, its black tail flicking in the wind.

"So how do we get them to the barn?" I ask. If Marcus asks me to jump on a horse and ride it to the ranch, I'm going to faint.

"Hop out," Marcus says. "I'm going to drive behind the horses and push them forward. Jennie will stand on one side of the horses and you'll stand on the other. We'll move them toward the barn. You just need to make sure they don't wander to the side."

"How do I do that?" *Without dying*, I want to add.

"Make yourself as big as you can."

"I'm five feet tall."

"Think big thoughts."

I get out of the side-by-side and walk to the right of the horses while Jennie stands to the left. Marcus tells me to stretch my arms out like a fence. He edges the side-by-side forward, and the horses skitter as he gets closer. I swallow hard, wondering when they'll bolt directly at me and stomp me into the dirt. That has to be at least a hundred damage points.

I can hear Jennie chant, "I am a wall. No horse will get through me. I am an impenetrable wall."

"Walk with them," Marcus advises. "Keep your arms out and they'll think you're a barrier."

My shoulders ache, but I do what Marcus says. We make slow progress as Marcus nudges the horses ahead with the side-by-side and they lazily make their way back toward the barn, mostly ignoring Jennie and me.

"Where'd you learn to take care of horses?" I ask Marcus as we continue over the ridge.

"I was part of a trail-riding club in Houston, where I grew up."

"Isn't Houston a big city? What's it doing with cowboys?"

Marcus smirks. "It's Texas."

"I bet you were amazing, Mr. Marcus," Jennie says. "Riding down the middle of the street, all big up on your horse like a superhero. Did you ride it to the grocery store? Did you buy your milk and eggs and then gallop back home, all the eggs scrambled in your bag?"

I laugh and lower my arms, but a brown horse

spots me and starts walking in my direction. I shoot my arms up in the air again, straining my muscles to make myself as imposing as possible.

"Do you miss it?" I ask Marcus, trying to distract myself from my aching arms. "I mean, do you miss getting to ride horses in the middle of a big city?"

Marcus grips the steering wheel of the side-by-side tighter as his jaw clenches. He takes a deep breath and relaxes. "My buddy Olstead used to ride with me, but it wasn't the same once he was gone. So now it's better for me out here. Quieter."

As the horses continue, I wish Beto and Yesi could see me. I'm more like a warrior rounding up wild blarg-mores than my player character mage, who would crouch behind a boulder and wait for them to take action. In The Forgotten Age, you roll the die to see in what order the players take their turns and make their decisions. I always hope for a low number so I don't have to go first.

"Watch that one," Marcus says, pulling me from The Forgotten Age and back to Rancho Espanto.

I notice a gray horse has edged itself out from the group and come closer to me on the right. A rock lands at the horse's feet and he startles, scampering in my direction.

"Stand firm and put your arms up!" Marcus shouts.

I'm going to pee my pants.

Shooting my arms in the air, I swallow hard and try to make myself as tall as possible. Squeezing my eyes shut, not wanting to witness the horse stampeding at me, I hear another rock land on the ground. I open my eyes and see yet another rock tumble toward the horse's hooves. I'm too busy watching the gray horse stomp toward me to look for the source of the flying rocks.

"Please stop, please stop," I mutter over and over to the horse, not wanting Marcus to see how scared I am. He's busy pushing the rest of the horses toward the barn with the side-by-side as Jennie walks with him.

Another rock flies to the ground next to the horse and he scampers closer to me. I stretch my arms as high as they'll go, feeling like I'm going to pull them out of their sockets. I squeeze my eyes shut again, waiting for the horse to slam into me with its wall of hard muscle and sharp bone.

Then I feel hot breath on my face.

I open my eyes and see the horse, inches from my nose. I take a deep breath but am still too afraid to lower my arms, no matter how much they're aching.

"Could you please go that way?" I whisper, and gesture toward the barn with my chin.

The horse stares at me and slowly turns.

"Keep moving forward, Alvarez," Marcus says. He's moved the other horses toward the barn. They must've realized where the hay is because they've picked up the pace and started trotting toward the horse pasture. Jennie claps her hands behind them and they move quicker toward the barn.

I take a step around the gray horse. It turns and faces the direction of the barn.

"Just start walking. He'll follow you," Marcus tells me. "He knows where the food is."

I walk toward the barn, the gray horse clomping behind me.

I hear Marcus chuckle. "You can put your arms down now."

"Oh," I say as my cheeks redden. So much for being a brave warrior.

I glance behind me and see the gray horse still following.

But past the horse, just over the ridge, I spot the man in the green sweater crouched behind a boulder, a rock clenched in his hand.

CHAPTER 7

THE ONLY THING worse than facing down a scared horse intent on stomping your pancreas into the dust?

Trying to find a seat by yourself in a small crowded dining hall.

I hold my tray in my hand and scan the rows of tables. I'm fine eating by myself, but with so many people in the dining hall, I'd be wedging myself between artists arguing over the best brand of oil paint and paleontologists debating which shovel is better.

I might as well be in the middle of an Eldervorn tavern, surrounded by brawling orclings and drunk blargmores.

As long as I don't see the man in the green sweater, I'll be fine. If I do, I'm gonna steal a can of green chilies from the Gearhart brothers and dump them over his head.

I don't know what in the babosan bomb his problem is with me. Did I kick his favorite pet puppy in another life? Did I eat the last peanut butter chip cookie his mom made? Being weird and yelling random things at me is one thing. I just finished sixth grade. That happened practically every day. But throwing rocks to try to get a horse to plant its hooves in my appendix is another.

I find a seat at a table in the corner and take a bite of one of the three peanut butter sandwiches I made, each sliced in three strips, just how Mom always made them. The chicken enchiladas the Gearhart brothers tried to pile on my plate seemed to have more green chilies than chicken.

"Hey, Rafa!" I hear a voice call from across the dining hall.

Jonas walks over to my table and sits down. His sandy brown hair is still sticking out in every direction, and his glasses have so many smudges on them I wonder if he can actually see me. How he and my "everything has to be perfect" dad became friends in college is beyond me.

"Mail call!" Jonas says, slapping three envelopes on the table. "These came for you today. You're lucky you got them. Must be some kind of mix-up at the post office. Half the letters in our bag were for Miss Maudie's Moose Rescue in Anchorage, Alaska."

I raise my eyebrow at Jonas as he shrugs. I take the envelopes and see letters from Beto, Yesi, and Mom. My thumb starts to push under the seal on Beto's letter, but Jonas taps his fingers on the table and says, "So, how's your first week at the ranch been? I heard you had an exciting day yesterday with the horses."

I think about the cows that disappeared in the canyon on our hike and the obnoxious man in the green sweater who yelled at me and tried to get me trampled by horses.

"Um . . . yeah. Some of the horses got out, but Jennie and I helped Marcus get them back in the corral."

Jonas smiles and plays with the knobs on the walkie-talkie hooked to his belt. "Look, Rafa, I know your dad said this was a punishment, but I hope that you'll learn things by being here. Make sure you do everything just like Marcus tells you. We can't have horses running loose all over the ranch. It's dangerous."

I look at Jonas's green eyes, barely visible behind the smudges on his glasses. He wipes his palms on his cargo pants and stares at me.

Wait. Does he think I had something to do with the horses getting out? Ño. That's not possible. It was . . .

My mind flashes to the man in the green sweater toying with the chain on the gate before he yelled at me. But how do I explain that to Jonas? The man doesn't even seem real.

I roll my shoulders and sit up straight. "Yes, sir," I tell him, wanting to change the subject from stampeding horses. "I'm actually learning a lot at the barn. A lot about poop. And all the forms it comes in."

Jonas slaps the table again, his expression softening. "Excrement is the best thing ever! Do you know how much you can learn about someone from their excrement?"

"Wait. Don't you mean 'something,' like an animal, not 'someone,' like a person?"

Jonas nods. "Oh, yeah, sure."

I stare at him and he winks. "Anyway, I'll leave you to your letters, your peanut butter sandwiches, and your poop. Don't forget what I said about listening to Marcus."

I tear into Beto's and Yesi's letters as Jonas walks over to a table of scientists and slaps them on the back.

In his letter, Beto tells me all about how he and Yesi can't convince enough people to join their group for The Forgotten Age so they've been working on perfecting their player characters, since it's pretty impossible to play the game with only two people. He's included a character sheet in his letter so I can work on mine. Yesi's letter mostly includes her plan to steal her sister's car, drive out to New Mexico all the way from Florida, and rescue me from what she thinks is a ranch filled with demons that want to snack on my liver.

Picking at the corners of the last envelope, I take a deep breath. I run my finger under the seal and pull out Mom's letter. It's typed, which I expected. She gets too tired to write sometimes.

¡Oye, Pollito!

How are things in the great state of New Mexico? Do they listen to Maluma out there? Or serve lechon con yuca? I mean, we have to have priorities, Pollito.

A smile tugs at my lips. Mom sounds like her old self.

You know those pincushions that your abuelita had that were shaped like a tomato? Ño ñaña, I think that's what I'm going to be for Halloween, since that's how I feel these days. The doctors decided . . .

I fold the letter back up quickly and shove it in the envelope. I don't want to read any more and concentrate on stacking the strips of peanut butter sandwich that I've made. But my hands shake and the bread tower topples over on my plate. I start counting my fingers as I wonder what Mom is doing right now. Is Dad making sure her favorite blanket to wrap up in is clean? Does he know that she likes it when I put it in the dryer for a few minutes to warm it up? Is he making sure to add a little almond extract to her chocolate protein shakes because they taste better that way?

I used to do all that for Mom. But now I'm here. And it's Dad's fault.

"Why are you eating a peanut butter sandwich for dinner?" a voice asks. I look up and see Jennie. "These chicken enchiladas are the greatest thing ever created by humans in the history of forever."

She and Ms. Kim sit across from me at the table.

"I don't want to lose my sense of taste from eating too many green chilies," I tell them.

"Well, these aren't that bad tonight. Normally the Gearhart brothers' food is like 'call the fire department, your esophagus has caught fire.' Which is weird with all these chilies in here. I shouldn't be able to feel my tongue. Like, it should just be flopping around in my mouth like a paralyzed slug."

Ms. Kim chokes on her mouthful of enchilada. "Sweetie. Slugs? Not while we're eating," she says, patting Jennie's hand.

Jennie opens her mouth to speak again, but before she can get her latest word flood out, her mom says, "So how are you liking the ranch? Has working in the barn gotten any better?"

I've just taken a large bite from my sandwich. The peanut butter glues my mouth shut, making me mumble. "It's okay, I guess. I'm learning enough new words each day to make your abuji really happy, that's for sure. *Stirrup, bit, rein.* Oh, and *manure*. So much manure. And I got to run the barn by myself today while Marcus was in Santa Fe . . . for an appointment."

Marcus went for a therapy session, but I don't know if I'm supposed to tell Jennie and Ms. Kim that. Guillermo never liked people knowing he was going to counseling, but I don't see what's so bad about saying you need to talk to someone.

Ms. Kim smiles as Jennie shovels another forkful of chili-covered enchiladas in her mouth.

"Mr. Marcus is the coolest person on the planet,"

Jennie says between chews. "Definitely the coolest person on the ranch. I love hanging out with him. I'd clean up the Mount Everest of elephant dung to get to work with him. Like, give me the biggest shovel right now."

Poking at the enchilada on her plate, Ms. Kim's smile grows. "He's very good at what he does."

"How long has he been working at the ranch? As long as you have?" I ask.

"Jennie and I have been here two years," Ms. Kim says. I think about Jennie telling me that her dad died two years ago, and I wonder how much their move to the ranch had to do with his death. "Marcus came just a couple of months after we did. Jonas said he applied through a veterans job program."

"Where did you guys live before here?" I ask, wondering if I should, if it'll make them upset to have to talk about Jennie's dad.

Ms. Kim clears her throat and rubs her thumb over the RK tattoo on her wrist. "We lived in Albuquerque, since my husband was teaching at the university there. I worked for the public library. But this is a nice change of pace for us."

She glances over at Jennie, who's staring at her plate of enchiladas. Ms. Kim reaches for Jennie's hand, but Jennie jerks it away.

"Did you know the old barn manager that Mr. Marcus replaced got scared off by ghosts?" Jennie says, tapping her fork on the table. "He couldn't take the tortured murder victims of the Arnoldson brothers haunting the barn and messing with the animals."

"Ño," I say, swallowing hard and wondering if ghosts can manipulate gate locks.

Ms. Kim nudges Jennie with her elbow. "That's not true and you know it. He said his knees hurt too much to do the job anymore so he went to live with his granddaughter in Colorado. I don't think any ghosts were involved at all."

Jennie shrugs and takes another large bite of enchiladas, a bit of green chili sticking to the side of her mouth.

I look past her and into the kitchen, where the Gearhart brothers are standing over a large tray of enchiladas. A buzz-cut brother stabs an enchilada and shoves the whole thing in his mouth, green sauce dripping down his chin. He shrugs as he chews and narrows his eyes at his two brothers as they hold cans labeled EIGHT ALARM GREEN CHILI FIRE SAUCE.

"Are those really not spicy? Like, at all?" I ask Jennie and Ms. Kim.

Jennie holds out a forkful of enchilada to me. "Try it. See for yourself. It's like eating a big mouthful of boiled potatoes."

I tentatively take a bite, waiting for my eyes to water and my throat to burn. I can feel the chilies in my mouth as I chew, but they don't taste anything like the lava-filled breakfast burrito Jennie gave me on my first day at Rancho Espanto. More like oatmeal that got left out too long after no one wanted to eat it.

Looking around the dining hall, I notice people poking around their plates with their folks, shrugging as they chew and pouring lakes of hot sauce on their enchiladas from the bottles on the tables. The murmuring gets louder as people start to argue about the unusually mild food. Something is going on with the Gearhart brothers' cooking, as if a mage cast a "no taste" spell.

"See?" Jennie says. "I told you so."

"It's a little weird, I guess," I say.

Jennie leans forward across the table, her eyes boring into me. "I have a theory," she whispers. "Rancho Espanto actually is haunted. Not 'fake stories by the Arnoldson brothers' haunted. But really and truly haunted."

I raise my eyebrows in disbelief but then think about what's happened to me since I arrived on the ranch. "What makes you think that?"

Jennie pushes her plate toward Ms. Kim, who's deep in conversation with the paleontologist sitting next to her. She takes a deep breath. "Well, it's obvious it's the earth babies finally come to life. The storm brought them, I'm sure of it."

"What in the world is an earth baby?" I ask as I watch two of the Gearhart brothers dump four cans of Eight Alarm Green Chili Fire Sauce on top of a tray of enchiladas.

Jennie flips a purple braid over her shoulder. "They're huge beasts with six feet and bodies covered in red hair. They're made from the clay around here. Sure, they started out as something the Arnoldson brothers just made up to keep people away from the area and all the cows they'd stolen. But somehow, their ghosts have brought the earth babies to life. I know it. And now their superpowers are starting to affect things."

Jennie holds up a forkful of tasteless enchilada to prove her wild point and winks at me. I can't tell if she's being serious with her story.

I think about the cows I saw in the canyon on my first hike here, or at least the cows I thought I saw. The memory starts to swirl and morph in my brain and suddenly the cows have rusty red fur and six hooves. I shake my head and blink, but the memory is immediately replaced by the image of the man in the green sweater yelling at me and throwing rocks. Maybe the cows are really Forgotten Age alosynths that morph into earth babies, or the other way around. Maybe I'm starting to get a headache.

Jennie leans even closer, her elbow on the table. I think any second she's going to crawl over our plates.

"It's the Arnoldson brothers. They want people off their land. And they've brought the earth babies to life to do it. I heard one of the scientists here say he found tracks that looked like Coelophysis, but they were . . . fresh. I don't think it was a dinosaur. It was the earth babies."

I bite my lip and think about what Jennie is telling me. "Do you know a lot more about the Arnoldson brothers? And these earth baby things?"

Jennie smirks. "I'm the daughter of a librarian. And of a history professor."

I pretend not to notice how she slightly deflates at the mention of her dad, her shoulders sagging and her lips pressed in a tight line. She sits back in her chair again.

I pause for a moment, chewing on the inside of my mouth and forming what I really want to ask. I think about the strange man I've seen telling me I can't be here, yelling at me to stay away, as if he wanted me off his land. Tossing my peanut butter sandwich back on my plate, I take a deep breath.

"Um, is there any chance one of the Arnoldson brothers wore a green sweater?"

CHAPTER 8

GHOSTS DON'T EXIST in The Forgotten Age. There are mages who can cast spells to prolong your life. There are warriors who can save you from the brink of death. There are bards who will tell your story long after you've stopped playing. But there are no ghosts.

Once you're dead, you're gone forever.

No more trips to the library, no more quesitos, no more arroz con pollo.

As I tie up my shoes to head to the barn the next morning, I think of everything I know about ghosts. And it's not a lot.

Jennie said she had no idea what color sweaters the Arnoldson brothers wore. I didn't feel cold when I first saw the man in the green sweater, but my stomach did flip-flop. So far, I think I'm the only one who's seen him. Could he be visible to me and no one else?

And if he is a ghost, why in the moldy mage mugwort does he seem so angry with me? I don't even want to be on his land. Why is he telling me to stay away and no one else?

Mom always told me that if I went out at night with wet hair, I'd die instantly from a cold. Apparently, every Cuban mother knows this is true. I'd usually shoot back that I'd haunt her as a wet, messy-haired ghoul. But even I didn't really believe that was true. Because ghosts aren't real.

Right?

I'm halfway to the barn from my room when I hear raised voices.

"I don't know what the problem is, man. He's never said anything to me. I didn't know he was having so much trouble."

I round the corner and see Marcus and Jonas standing at the entrance to the barn. Jonas grips a paper while Marcus shakes his head, clenching his fists with his lips sealed in a tight line.

"Well, apparently he hates this place. He told me as much right here," Jonas says, gesturing with the paper in his hand.

Marcus nods, his chest heaving. But he doesn't say anything.

Jonas drops his hand when he sees me. "Rafa, we should chat," he says as I approach.

I touch my thumb to each of my fingers, counting them over and over in my head. I'm not sure what they're talking about, but my stomach rumbles anyway.

Jonas holds out the paper to me. "I got your note. I didn't realize you were so unhappy here. And while I appreciate your confession, this is serious business."

What in the babosan bomb is he talking about?

My hand shakes as I take the paper from Jonas and read.

I don't like it here. The guy in the barn is mean to me. So that's why I let the horses out. I figured if I messed up, you'd send me home. I really want to go home.—Rafa

I look from Jonas to Marcus with wide eyes. "I . . . I didn't write this," I stammer.

Examining the paper again, I stare at the messy handwriting. The way whoever wrote it was in such a hurry, they joined half the letters in fake cursive and didn't bother to dot their *i*'s.

It's how I write. This is my handwriting. How is this possible? Is some Forgotten Age alosynth pretending to be me?

"Really?" Marcus says, clearing his throat.

I shake my head. "I promise. I don't know what's going on, but this isn't me. I didn't write this. And I didn't let the horses out."

Jonas puts his hand on my shoulder. "I want to believe you, Rafa. I really do. But if you are telling the truth—"

"I am," I blurt out before I can stop myself.

Jonas takes a deep breath and pushes his glasses up the bridge of his nose. "Just be careful. If anything else happens, we'll have to have a much more serious conversation. I know your dad would expect that."

Before I can respond, Jonas tucks the letter in his pocket and heads off toward the administration building.

I stare at Marcus, who's standing like a statue, fists clenched. Before I can say anything, he turns on his heel and marches into his office. After a moment, I hear music coming from inside.

The horses huff and scratch their hooves on the

floor. Shoving my hands in my pockets, I walk to Marcus's office and lean against the doorframe.

"You listen to Taylor Swift?" I ask, not knowing what to say about the letter or Jonas.

Marcus takes a deep breath. My eyes trail to his arms, where I notice scars zigzagging under his elbows. He pulls on the sides of his dusty T-shirt at the shoulders, as if he's repositioning a backpack he's not wearing.

"That girl calms me down," he says.

I mutter, "It wasn't me, you know. I didn't leave the gate open. I'm sorry, but I don't know how the horses got out. And I didn't write that letter. Why would I call you 'the guy in the barn'? I know your name."

I swallow hard, shoving down all the frustration building in my throat as I count my fingers, digging my thumbnail into each pad.

Marcus takes another deep breath and seems to soften. "I know, Alvarez. We haven't known each other long, but I'm good at sizing folks up. I know you're not like that."

"But you didn't say anything to Jonas. You didn't tell him it wasn't me."

Marcus scratches his chin. "He came flying at me before I'd even had my coffee. Started telling me I had to be nicer to you because you were unhappy. I was trying my hardest not to say something I would regret. Or do anything I couldn't take back."

Marcus makes his coffee, offering me a cup, which I quickly decline.

My stomach is already in knots. I don't need it exploding into my liver because of his rancid concoction.

After downing his coffee in one gulp, Marcus turns off his music and nods at me.

Time for work.

We march over to the pile of hay behind the barn and begin distributing a flake to each of the horses. I glance at the gate along the horse pasture, the lock secured around the chains. Marcus doesn't say anything as we work, his eyes clouded from his thoughts. He keeps tugging at the shoulders of his T-shirt.

I clear my throat, wanting to distract myself from thinking about the weird note confessing that I let the horses out, remembering the man in the green sweater standing at the gate and messing with the lock. I grab a flake of hay, grateful it makes me stop counting my fingers. "So, I figured out your secret power," I tell Marcus, dumping the hay in Frankie's feeder.

Marcus raises an eyebrow but stays silent.

"In The Forgotten Age, everyone has a secret power. Yours is definitely 'constitution.'" I pick up another flake in my arms and face Marcus, bits of hay falling to the floor. "You can withstand any poison attack. You're completely immune to it."

Marcus smirks, dumping a flake of hay in Mia's feeder. "Why is that my power?"

"You get it from your coffee. If you can survive drinking that, you can survive anything." I dump a flake of hay in Jiji's stall and stand triumphantly in front of Marcus, waiting for him to bask in the glory of my revelation.

A low chuckle erupts from his throat. "You're never gonna let the coffee thing go, are you, Alvarez?"

"Never. Cuban Americans have very strong opinions about coffee." At least that's what Mom always used to say as she watched her dark concoction brew in the morning, impatiently tapping her fingers on the kitchen counter.

But she doesn't have the stomach for her favorite beverage anymore.

Marcus grabs gloves from the top of a barrel and shoves them on his hands with more force than seems necessary. His eyes cloud over once again.

"So coffee makes me survive anything?" He huffs. "Maybe I survived things I'm not supposed to. That ever happened in your game?"

I sit on a bale of hay and brush dirt off my jeans. "One time Beto, Yesi, and I were playing, and we got stuck in the dungeons of Anderwilde. The orcling guards were closing in, and we were sure they were going to fry our guts in runtberry soup. Yesi kept rolling a three, sending us deeper and deeper into the dungeon instead of up the steps and out to safety. We were about to give up, when my mom brought down some quesitos for us to eat."

"What's a quesito?" Marcus asks, adjusting the gloves on his hands and flexing his fingers.

"It's sweetened cream cheese rolled up in puff pastry and sprinkled with sugar. Pretty much the greatest food invention ever, right behind guava pastelitos. You don't know what a quesito is?"

Marcus shakes his head.

I shrug. "Ño. I feel bad for your childhood," I tell him, winking.

Marcus rolls his eyes. "So what happened in this dungeon place you were stuck in? You get fried or roasted or whatever?"

I shake my head. "So we devoured Mom's quesitos, which I'm pretty sure have magical properties, and the next time Yesi rolled, she got a twenty. That never happens. It was a quesito miracle. We ran right out of the dungeon and away to safety."

"Sounds like you need to eat your mom's cooking more often."

I look down at my shoes and scuff my feet along the floor, leaving lines of dirt along bits of hay. "She doesn't have energy to cook anymore. It's been takeout and cream-based casseroles from people at church for the past six months."

Marcus looks me up and down and I squirm under his stare. His gaze softens. "I've had those casseroles. Not much seasoning. And forget remembering what dish belonged to what person."

I swallow hard. "You've gotten those casseroles a lot?"

Marcus stares at me directly. "People forget food doesn't bring back the dead."

Heat rises to my cheeks, and I count my fingers again. Marcus notices and shakes his head. He thinks for a moment and then slaps his knee, startling me. "I think I figured out your secret superpower."

I look at him and raise my eyebrow. "Oh, really? What is it?"

"I'm thinking you're one of those kids who likes to tell stories and ask their teacher distracting questions in class to get them off track so they don't actually assign any work."

Busted.

"Well, bad news, Alvarez," Marcus says, grabbing a rake from the wall of the barn and handing it to me. "Time for everyone's favorite chore—mucking out stalls."

I shake my head. "No way scooping poop is anyone's favorite chore. That's a certified fact."

I spend the next two hours cleaning out each horse's stall, making sure there's no manure hiding under the hay on the floor. It gets more tiring with each stall, as if the horses are mages, casting spells to make their poop weigh more than a thousand orclings. My back hurts and my shoulders feel like they're going to drop from their sockets. But at least all the work keeps me from thinking about the strange letter and the man in the green sweater who seems determined to make my life miserable.

When I finish, I trudge to the barn office, where I hear Marcus inside. Standing in the doorway, I see him with his left foot on the seat of his chair. The leg of his pants is pulled above his knee as he rubs cream on a long, snaking scar that cuts across his calf.

I clear my throat and Marcus looks up. He yanks the leg of his pants down and stands.

"You don't need to ask me about that, Alvarez," he mumbles, his eyes dark as he frowns.

I take a deep breath, the palms of my hands still burning from using the rake. Beto's brother, Guillermo, has a scar that starts in the middle of his chin and runs along his jawline. He won't tell us how it happened, so Beto just says Guillermo got it fighting blargmores.

"Fine. And you don't need to ask me about this," I say, pointing to the scar that sits right above my left eyebrow.

Marcus squints at my forehead.

"I'm serious. Don't ask me," I tell him, holding my hands up in surrender. My shoulders, sore from all the stall raking, scream for me to put my arms down. "You don't need to know that I valiantly fought a doorknob when I was five. It tried to damage me permanently, but I prevailed."

Marcus smirks. "You ran into a doorknob?"

"Yes."

"You ran directly into a closed door?"

"Yes. I did."

Chuckling, Marcus shoves the tube of cream into his desk. "You're a true warrior, Alvarez."

I lift my chin, basking in Marcus's statement.

Pointing at me, Marcus says, "And this warrior is done for the day. So go back to your room. And maybe shower since you smell like Frankie didn't like his last meal."

I nod and sniff my shirt. It smells like the section of the Hedor Swamps with rotting orcling carcasses. I walk from the barn and head toward my room until I hear shouts coming from down the path. Raised voices sound like they're coming from the direction of the library. Jogging that way, my back mutinies and tries to throw me on the ground.

I reach the patio of the library and hear Jennie's high-pitched voice. "This is going to take forever to clean up! I can't believe he did this!"

I walk through the door of the library and stop in my tracks. It looks like a wild blargmore smashed its scaly body into every shelf. Books lay thrown across the floor, entire shelves pulled off the wall and onto the ground.

Ms. Kim turns and looks at me, her arms full of books and her hair messy across her face. "Rafa . . . why did you . . . ?" she stammers.

"What happened?" I ask.

Jennie drops the books in her arms on the floor and puts her hands on her hips. "Don't you already know? Why are you acting surprised?"

I scan the books scattered at Jennie's feet. "What are you talking about?"

Jennie sighs and tosses a purple braid over her shoulder. "You know if you were looking for a book, you could've just asked. That's what librarians are for! I don't understand why you would mess everything up."

I step back from Jennie and glance from her to Ms.

Kim. I drop my gaze, unable to look Ms. Kim in the eye. She walks toward me, setting the books in her arms on a cart. Placing her hand on my shoulder, she says, "Jonas said there's a lot going on with you, but this isn't the way to handle it, Rafa. This is a big mess that's going to take a long time to clean up. I don't know why you felt the need to do this, but the least you can do is help us fix this."

I swallow hard, tears starting to prick the corners of my eyes. "Why do you think it was me? I really didn't do this," I say.

Jennie crosses her arms, eyeing me suspiciously. "That's not what I heard. Everyone is saying you let the horses at the barn out, and now this. What's going on with you?"

I stomp my foot on the floor. "I didn't do that, either. Why does everybody think I'm doing all these terrible things? It wasn't me!"

Chewing on the inside of her mouth, Jennie steps closer to me. "Well, someone ratted you out. They saw you come in here this morning and destroy everything. What do you have against books, anyways? I thought you liked them. I thought you liked us!"

I stomp again, clenching my fists at my side. "I didn't do this!"

"But that's not what the guy in the green sweater said. That guy you were asking about at dinner," Jennie says as she looks me up and down. "He saw you do everything. He said you unlocked the gate at the barn and messed everything up here this morning."

Ms. Kim squeezes my shoulder. "He didn't know why you did it, either, but he saw you do everything. Do you think maybe it's too much for you to be here? Should I talk to Jonas about seeing if you should just go home?"

I take a deep breath. "A guy in a green sweater?" I ask.

"Yeah," Jennie says, shoving her hands in her pockets. "So what? You gonna tell me it was really the Arnoldson brothers and their earth babies? Geez, I was mostly kidding when I told you about them."

I want to defend myself, but I know they won't believe me.

When I look down at the book at my feet, I see it flipped open to a page about Rancho Espanto. In a smudged photograph, several men stand in front of a tree. I gasp as I look at its branches and see a man hanging from the end of a rope, his neck twisted at an unnatural angle.

Even though the colors in the photograph are faded, the dead man's sweater is definitely green.

CHAPTER 9

I SPENT TWO hours helping Ms. Kim and Jennie fix the shelves and straighten up all the books in the library. Jennie didn't say a word to me as we worked, which I think is probably some kind of record for her. The bulging vein in her forehead, peeking out from under her purple bangs, looked like it grew bigger with each book she shoved back on a shelf.

I think I would've preferred her yelling at me to the silence.

I trudge to the dining hall after we finish fixing everything, ready to quickly make a peanut butter sandwich and take it back to my room to eat.

"Hey, kid," the buzz-cut Gearhart brother calls to me as I'm pulling two slices of bread out of a bag. "C'mere."

I walk over to him and raise my eyebrow when he holds out a large spoon piled with green chili stew.

"Eat this." Buzz-Cut Gearhart shoves the spoon an inch from my face.

"Excuse me?"

"I got a theory, kid. Prove me right."

I just want to go to my room, away from everyone who thinks I let horses out and messed up the books in the library. Taking the spoon from Buzz-Cut Gearhart, I shove the green chili stew in my mouth. I can taste the chunks of pork and potatoes drowning in chilies, but it isn't spicy at all.

Buzz-Cut Gearhart stares at me with narrowed eyes as I swallow. He crosses his arms as I set the spoon on the metal table between us.

"Well, rat butt. I'm wrong."

From behind him, Glasses Gearhart cackles as he stirs a large pot on the stove. "You hear that, boys? He admitted he was wrong. Mark the date!"

I start to turn from him and back to making my sandwich, when Buzz-Cut Gearhart says, "Don't you want to know what I was wrong about?"

Honestly? No.

He doesn't wait for me to answer. "You were the last person to arrive on the ranch before our food got

107

all out of sorts like a six-toed cat. I told the boys you brought bad karma to the ranch, what with everything going sideways since you got here. But that maybe you weren't affected by your own powers and the food would still be spicy for you. I guess I was wrong about that part."

I don't have the energy to defend myself anymore. I nod and shrug, turning away from Buzz-Cut Gearhart, but not before he reaches to a small bowl on the table and throws a pinch of salt in my face.

I sputter. "Um, why?"

"That's how we handle cursed things, you know," he replies.

I make my sandwich as fast as I can before the Gearhart brothers can decide how else they'll try to get rid of the bad luck they think I've brought to the ranch. I can't help but notice the eyes staring at me in the dining hall as I leave, and one silver-haired woman who mutters, "I wonder if it was him that messed up my painting. It looked completely different this morning."

Running back to my room, I toss the book with the photo of the Arnoldson brother that I took from the library. I don't have the stomach to look at the picture again or to eat my sandwich.

Resting my head in my hands as I sit on my bed, I think about the fake letter that said I wanted to go home. And Ms. Kim who suggested the same thing.

I guess things would be better at home. I'd have Mom's arroz con pollo instead of the Gearhart brothers' green chili concoctions. I'd have afternoons in the library with Beto and Yesi instead of hours scooping horse poop.

Except Mom's too tired to make arroz con pollo anymore. And Dad says I can't go to the library so I can be home in case Mom needs anything.

Home isn't home anymore.

So I'm stuck in Rancho Espanto. With everyone thinking I'm doing terrible things to mess everything up. And a ghost Arnoldson brother who seems to have it out for me and wants me off his land.

Ño, what if Dad decides that a month isn't long enough for my punishment and he makes me stay here all summer? And I have to eat only peanut butter sandwiches for two more months? And the man in the green sweater decides that I'd make great food for the pack of earth babies he is using to control things on the ranch?

I pull my twenty-sided die out of my pocket. "Is the man in the green sweater a ghost haunting me?"

I roll the die and it lands on ten. That's not really a yes or a no. I pull the book I got from the library, *The History of Northeastern New Mexico*, and flip to the index at the back. I scan for entries about Rancho Espanto or the Arnoldson brothers. There's an entry for Rancho Espanto and I flip to the page listed in the index.

But it doesn't give me much to go on. All it says is that Rancho Espanto was won by a new owner in the 1920s in a game of poker. Which I already knew because Jennie told me the first day I met her.

I shut the book and press my hands on the cover. I close my eyes, hoping to cast a spell like a mage so that the next time I open the book, it tells me exactly who the man in the green sweater is and what he wants with me.

Grabbing another library book, I trace my fingers over *Ghosts on the Ranch*, printed on its spine. I flip to the index in the back, just like I did with the other book, and look up the Arnoldson brothers. Turning to the page listed, I read that their names were Bartlett and Ephram. Most of the information is what I already learned from Jennie—that the brothers stole cattle, hid them in the canyons around the ranch, and spread rumors about ghosts, earth babies, and monster snakes so people would stay away. But there's some new information as well. I learn that it was Bartlett who killed Ephram after they argued over some gold they had stolen. So that means Bartlett is the one in the green sweater hanging from the tree in the photograph.

Is he the one who's been stomping around the ranch, messing things up and getting me blamed so I'll get off his land?

Under the photograph, which I cover with my hand so I don't have to look at it, I read more about the Arnoldson brothers. About how travelers would swear they could hear screaming coming over the ridges and how Ephram's wife fled the area with her child after he died, swearing Bartlett was possessed.

My stomach rolls and I slam the book shut.

I spot Señor Spider creeping across my floor, headed

for my shoes. "Hey, bro. You know much about ghosts, particularly potential serial killer ghosts? I mean, you're not really a ghost spider, are you?" I ask.

I half expect him to look straight at me with his eight eyes and answer. That would actually be more helpful than what I've got now.

Mom always says the solution to any problem lies at the bottom of a bag of plantain chips. I used to doubt that particular piece of advice, especially since all her advice seemed to be food related, until I realized that I couldn't count my fingers anxiously if they were picking out chips from the bag.

I chew on the inside of my mouth and rummage through my suitcase. I pull out a shoebox from my suitcase and open it, revealing sesame candy, Twizzlers, and, best of all, small bags of plantain chips. Mom left Dad a list of snacks for him to buy at Publix so I could take them to New Mexico. Dad grumbled that I was being punished and didn't need snacks. Mom gave him her most pathetic look, which isn't hard to conjure these days, and said she wouldn't be able to focus on her treatment if she was worried about me going hungry.

My breath hitches in my throat and I squeeze my eyes shut, trying to think of something else quickly to get rid of the image of Mom hooked up to needles and tubes, surrounded by beeping machines.

Blargmores, alimancitas, orclings . . .

I shake my head and set a bag of plantain chips and two sesame candies on the nightstand next to my bed, eyeing Señor Spider on the floor to make sure he doesn't think I'm leaving out treats for him.

I'll need help if I'm going to catch Bartlett Arnold-son, the ghost man in the green sweater. And I know just how to get it.

When I head to the barn the next morning, there's a note on the door of Marcus's office. It just says *Santa Fe.*

That means he's in Santa Fe for his therapy appointment today. I breathe a sigh of relief. I won't have to come up with some twisted tale of why I can't work with him all day.

Because I have other plans.

I muck out all the stalls as quickly as I can. *Muck* is definitely the right term, since that's exactly what poop and hay look like when they get mixed together.

I use the hose to refill all the water troughs in the stalls and give a flake of hay to each horse. I even take out Wattson, Jiji, Mia, and Frankie and brush them down with a curry brush, spraying each of them with fly spray when I'm finished.

If only Beto and Yesi could see me now. They would declare that I'd definitely reached my peak form as a mage, with my ability to make horses do my bidding.

I just want to do a good job for Marcus so that he'll have one less thing to worry about while he's at his therapy session in Santa Fe.

When I finish with all my barn chores, it's a little after lunchtime. I'm sweatier than I'd like and I'm pretty sure I smell like the muck I scooped out of the stalls.

But I still have an important mission to complete.

I leave the barn and head down the path toward the library. When I enter, I'm relieved to see it hasn't been mysteriously destroyed again. All the books are still on their shelves. I spot Ms. Kim in her office, on the phone. She smiles at me cautiously and my stomach flip-flops. As I walk to the graphic novel section in the back, I hear Ms. Kim say into the phone, "There's no way your research materials turned into manga. I have no idea what you're talking about."

I hear the music as soon as I walk farther into the library. Growling, heavy drums and screaming electric guitars. When I round the corner to where the graphic novels are, I spot Jennie, jumping up and down. She's banging her head from side to side, her purple braids flying. A laptop sits on the table in front of her, blasting heavy metal music.

I clear my throat and Jennie stops dancing, hitting the space bar on the laptop to pause the music.

I shove my hands in my pockets so she won't see me counting my fingers. "So what are you listening to?" I ask as casually as possible, unsure if she'll speak to me after yesterday.

Flinging a braid over her shoulder, Jennie huffs. "It's a Swedish metal band that sings about historical events. This one's about the Night Witches. Did you know they used plywood-and-canvas planes and dropped bombs on the Nazis in World War II? They flew at night and their planes sounded like swooshing brooms. That's how they got their name. Pretty much the coolest ladies ever in the history of cool ladies."

Grinning, I relax a little. It's a good sign that Jennie is back to her no-holding-back with me. "That seems like . . . a lot."

Jennie shrugs. "My dad was the one who got me into this band. He used to play their songs at the beginning of his classes."

She opens her mouth like she's going to say more but then closes it, reaching out and shutting the laptop instead.

Looking me up and down, Jennie says, "Did you finish early in the barn?"

I sit in the chair next to her and pull some sesame candies and a bag of plantain chips out of my jacket pocket.

"I thought I should introduce you to the best Cuban snacks in the world instead," I tell her, nudging the treats across the table in her direction. Mom always used to bribe me with snacks. I learned from the master.

Jennie's eyes grow big, but she bites her lip and

clenches her fists. I can tell she's trying to pretend she's not interested in my offering. I take one of the sesame candies and unwrap it. Biting down on the candy, I chew and roll my eyes.

"Ño, this is the absolute best. Sesame seeds mixed with sugar syrup. Your honey twists are good, but this is sticky perfection."

Jennie sighs and holds her hand out to me. I give her a sesame candy, which she quickly unwraps and pops in her mouth. A smile breaks out on her face as she chews.

I take the bag of plantain chips and open it, holding them out to her. "If you think that's good, you should try these. I could eat my weight in plantain chips every day."

Jennie takes two chips from the bag and shoves them in her mouth. The smile on her face grows bigger as she reaches in the bag and takes a handful of chips.

"Okay, I'm a little mad at you," Jennie says between chews.

I grip the edge of my chair, ready for her to launch into a verbal assault, accusing me of wrecking the library all over again.

She swallows and wipes the crumbs from her mouth. "You never told me Cuban snacks were, like, the best thing ever on this planet. You've had these with you the entire time and you never shared them with me? Holding back snacks is, like, the worst offense anyone could ever do. And these are amazing. The salty and sweet all mixed together? I want to marry them. Like, 'I now pronounce you person and snacks forever and ever.'"

I bite my lip to keep from cackling. Relieved that Jennie seems to have forgiven yesterday's incident, I tell her, "I need your help with something."

Brushing the crumbs off her jeans, Jennie looks me directly in the eye. "Name it. You give me more of these awesome Cuban snacks and I'll help you round up every single green chili in the state of New Mexico and launch them into the moon."

I shake my head. "Actually," I tell her, "I need you to help me catch a ghost."

CHAPTER 10

ONE TIME WHEN I was five, El Cucú lived in my closet. I was certain this boogeyman with sharp teeth and long fingernails was going to suck out my eyeballs once he got done eating all the shirts hanging in my closet.

I told Mom, but she didn't really believe me. Still, she helped me set up a Cucú Catcher, which was basically an old white laundry basket with a string attached to the end that I could pull and trap El Cucú.

As Jennie chews on more plantain chips, crumbs falling onto her teal University of New Mexico hoodie, I hope she believes me enough to set up our own Cucú Catcher. I tell her all about Bartlett Arnoldson and how I think he's trying to get me kicked off his land. I swallow hard when I tell her about the photo of him hanging from a tree and how not only is he wearing a green sweater, but he has dark floppy hair and a scar across his eyebrow just like the man I've seen around the ranch.

Jennie narrows her eyes at me and pauses, grabbing another sesame candy when I tell her I think Bartlett is the man who unlocked the gate at the barn, letting the horses out. And that he was actually the one who destroyed the library. Not a blargmore, and definitely not me. I leave out the ghost cows and that somehow I think he's responsible for the Gearhart brothers' oddly unspicy food.

I sit and wait for Jennie's reaction after I'm done, counting my fingers over and over as my palms sweat. She takes a deep breath, and I brace myself, expecting her to tell me the dry heat has fried my brain. That I'm as reasonable and intelligent as an alimancita rolling in Hedor Swamps mud.

Brushing crumbs from her lap, Jennie finally says, "Oh my god, you're being haunted by a ghost. That is, like, the coolest thing ever. I think you'll definitely win the 'what I did this summer' essay when you go back to school. How many kids are gonna be able to say they were terrorized by the spirit world in the middle of New Mexico? I might be slightly jealous. I mean, I saw him, too, when he tried to get Mom and me to think you messed up the library, but he's actually haunting you. So amazing."

I cough and a smirk grows on my lips. "I'm glad my mental torment amuses you."

Jennie stands up and grabs my hand. Pulling me into another part of the library, she continues her word flood. "No, but seriously. I was supposed to reorganize the photography section today. Like, hello, thank you, would I rather make sure the tiniest decimals are in the correct order or do I want to hunt a ghost? If the answer isn't obvious, then maybe you got kicked in the head by one of the horses."

We stand in front of a shelf of books as Jennie scans their spines.

"So in the three seconds from when I told you what was happening and now, you have a plan?" I ask.

Jennie bites her lip and nods, pulling a book from the shelf. She tucks it under her arm and grabs my hand again, dragging me toward her mother's office. Practically tossing me into the chair in front of Ms. Kim's computer, Jennie jiggles the computer mouse, making the monitor light up.

"We're going to combine the two greatest forces on the face of the earth," she declares.

"Plantain chips and honey twists?"

Cackling, Jennie shakes her head. "No, but save that one for later. Definite possibilities there. We're combining the power of paper in all its pulpy and inky glory," she says, fanning through the pages of her book, "with the power of technology and all its glitchy, digital might."

I purse my lips and raise my eyebrows, giving Jennie a confused look.

An exasperated sigh erupts from her throat and she smacks her forehead. "Seriously, Rafa. I don't have crayons and finger paint to explain this to you properly. But here's the basics. You need help finding the ghost man in the green sweater so he'll stop making things go wrong on the ranch and getting you blamed. We can be pretty sure the ghost man is Bartlett Arnoldson, given their similarities. Jonas told me once that Bartlett had a cabin somewhere on the ranch. We find the cabin, we find Bartlett. Don't ghosts usually haunt their old stomping grounds?"

Jennie leans over the computer and pulls up an

internet browser. It takes a while to load, and I suspect the internet service in the library is less than lightning speed.

"See if you can find maps of the area online and I'll look for maps in the library books," Jennie says, sharply nodding her head like we just struck a deal. She leaves Ms. Kim's office and I see her scan more shelves, pulling out additional books and setting them on a table.

I settle myself in front of the computer, wondering what I should search for to figure out where Bartlett's cabin might be. And how to avoid thirty-foot snakes, earth babies, and whatever else might be out there. I really wish my current situation came with a player handbook, like The Forgotten Age. That way I could just flip to the right page and it would outline "What to do when faced with a terrorizing ghost."

I type *maps* into the search engine and I can practically hear my sixth-grade English teacher squawking about using specific search terms. Especially when the first thing that pops up says "Multidisciplinary Association for Psychedelic Studies." Definitely not what I need. I type in *land maps*, and a link for the

Bureau of Land Management pops up. That sounds a little more legitimate.

I keep searching, zooming in and out on maps, clicking around the website until something remotely useful pops up. My eyes wander as my thoughts swirl and land on a photograph in a frame next to the computer. It's of Ms. Kim and Jennie at what looks like the Grand Canyon, standing next to a man wearing the same teal University of New Mexico hoodie that Jennie seems to wear every other day.

This must be Jennie's dad. He looks Korean like Ms. Kim and Jennie, but I don't want to assume anyone's background just by their appearance. He has a welcoming smile on his face that matches the grins on Ms. Kim's and Jennie's faces. Jennie is grabbing on to her dad's sweatshirt and leaning toward the canyon, as if she's pretending she's going to jump in. I trace my fingers over the firm grip that Jennie's dad has on her arm in the picture, like he'd never let anything happen to her.

I wonder when this picture was taken. Jennie's hair is dark brown like mine instead of purple, and she's a lot shorter than she is now. How long after this trip did Jennie's dad die? I look at their smiling faces and lit-up eyes, wondering if they had any idea what was going to happen. If they could sense what was waiting for them around the corner.

Would they want to be able to see into the future and know what was going to happen so they could prepare themselves? Or would they rather just be happy clinging to each other in this moment?

"Find anything?" Jennie asks, popping into the office and startling me.

"Um, not really," I say, clearing my throat and shaking my head.

"Well, no worries, because I think I've found it," Jennie says, grabbing my hand and pulling me to the table where she piled all her books. She pushes a stack of books aside and smacks a map down on the table.

"My eyes were almost bleeding going through all these books. Dead end after dead end. But then I had the most brilliant idea. Like, congratulations to me, I'm a genius. And it wasn't in any of these books. It was here," Jennie says, pointing at a folded brochure on the table that says *Rancho Espanto Hiking Trails: Visitor's Map.*

"You found what we need in there? Because all I really found on the computer was the highest elevation in New Mexico and where you can argue with the government about your property taxes."

Jennie rolls her eyes. "Wheeler Peak and the tax assessor's office. Duh. Everyone knows that. But this brochure shows all the trails around the ranch. I was looking at it and noticed that one of the trails kind of stands out. In like an 'abandon hope, all ye who enter here' way."

"That sounds like something we would want to avoid."

"We're already hunting a ghost. It's too late to avoid things," Jennie states, flipping open the brochure. She runs her finger over a long squiggly line that seems to circle the entire ranch. "And this Cauldron Mesa trail is something practically everyone on the ranch has told me to avoid. Mom says it's too long, Marcus says it's too narrow and steep. Jonas says it's an easy twelve miles, but his is maybe not the best opinion. There's one spot on the trail that has an old stone cabin, but no one is supposed to go near it. I think that might be what we're looking for. Especially since I heard Jonas say yesterday that some hikers swore up and down they saw a snake as big as a car near that cabin."

"Were they just making things up?"

Jennie shrugs. "Who knows? They said it had four sets of wings. Jonas told them to get off the ranch."

I bite my lip and shove my hands in the pockets of my shorts. "Forgetting the possible Forgotten Age creature lurking near this cabin, we're really gonna hike twelve miles to a stone cabin so we can possibly run into a serial killer ghost?"

Jennie shrugs. "If we start here," she says, pointing to one end of the trail, "it's only four miles to the cabin."

"Ño. Only."

"We should leave tomorrow morning. It's too late to start out now. We'd fry in the sun at this point. Like, our eyeballs would turn into hard-boiled eggs."

I nod and chew on the side of my mouth. "Do you think I could use your mom's computer one more time? I want to email Beto and Yesi about everything. They'll think I've finally perfected a new thief character and I'm going on a trek through the Yermola Wasteland."

"And I'm your warrior bodyguard who makes sure rattlesnakes don't bite your earlobes. But, yeah, go for it on Mom's computer. I've got to put these books back anyways. Mom'll toss me up in a tree like that alimancita you asked about if I leave a mess here. Like, launch me straight into the branches."

When I walk back to Ms. Kim's office, she's nowhere to be seen, so I sit in front of the computer. Clicking open my email, I fire off a message to Beto and Yesi, telling them all about the piles of horse poop I have to scoop, the fiery green chilies I used to have to avoid that are now as spicy as milk, and end with a quick "by the way, I think I'm being haunted by the ghost of a cattle-stealing serial killer."

I smirk as I imagine Yesi stomping immediately onto a plane and flying all the way out to New Mexico so she can charge up the entire Cauldron Mesa trail and slap Bartlett Arnoldson right in his face.

After I hit send on the email, the cursor hovers over the NEW MESSAGE button. I tap my foot on the floor as the light over Ms. Kim's desk buzzes. I click the mouse and type Mom's email address before I can change my mind.

Hi, Mom. How are you?

Delete.

Hey. I miss you.

Delete.

Please tell me what to do. Please get better. Please don't leave me alone.

Delete.

Delete.

Delete.

CHAPTER 11

I WAKE UP the next morning ready to enact the Great Plan. Beto would be proud of me. Hopefully this will go better than his Great Big Idea and won't end with me being drowned in green chili sauce while earth babies nibble my toes.

I can't even begin to guess how many damage points that would be.

Standing in front of the mirror in my bathroom, I turn on the faucet as hot as it will go. I wince as I wet my hands and splash the burning water on my face. My cheeks redden and my skin immediately looks flushed. I run my fingers through my hair, making it stick out in every direction.

Once I'm finished perfecting my appearance, I slip my feet into my shoes halfway, stepping on the backs of the heels. Trudging to the barn, I wrap my arms around my waist and groan.

An innocent bystander might think that Rancho

Espanto was suddenly overrun by the reanimated corpse of Bartlett Arnoldson, but it's just me, Rafa Alvarez, architect of the Great Plan.

I squeeze my eyes shut and shake my head when the thought of Marcus completely not believing me floods my brain. I don't want to picture his disappointed look and his hands on his hips as he banishes me from the ranch for lying to him.

This plan had better work.

If it doesn't, Marcus will kick me off the ranch while singing Taylor Swift and throwing my underwear in the dirt.

"Whoa, Alvarez," Marcus says when he sees me. He sets down his rake and looks me up and down. "You all right there?"

I make a big show of struggling to swallow as I breathe hard, my chest heaving.

"Gearhart . . . brothers . . ." I sigh, wiping my forehead. "Their food . . . bathroom . . . all night."

Marcus steps toward me and puts the back of his hand on my cheek. "Ouch. Their food hits hard even when it isn't spicy. You don't look so great. You sure you can work today?"

I swallow the grin that tries to creep across my

131

face. Slowly shaking my head, I mutter, "No, need to help . . . have to work . . . I can do it."

I stumble over to the bales of hay and slowly lift my arms to get a flake for the horses. I make a loud wrenching sound and double over, holding my stomach.

I know I'm a liar. But on the list of Urgent Things That Need Taking Care Of, scooping Jiji's poop ranks way below getting the ghost of Bartlett Arnoldson to stop wreaking havoc on the ranch and blaming me.

"Yeah, no horse wants to eat vomit hay," Marcus says, coming over and putting his hand on my back. "Why don't you rest today and we can just get back to it tomorrow?"

Turning to face Marcus, I plaster my most pathetic look on my face, drooping my eyes and leaving my mouth hanging half open, a look I learned from Mom. "Are you . . . sure?"

Marcus nods. "Gearharts have made everybody on the ranch feel like that at least once. Sometimes their cooking makes me crave a jambalaya MRE. Which is the worst flavor military ration. I was wondering when it was going to be your turn, especially since their food is worse than normal, with the zero spice, I mean."

Mom says liars are worse than the caca that covers your car when you park under a poinciana tree in the Publix parking lot.

I don't want to lie to Marcus. I actually like him a lot. He reminds me of Guillermo and isn't fazed when I go off on a worst-case-scenario tangent or when I don't want to talk about home.

Marcus seems to have a lot he doesn't want to talk about, either.

"Take it easy today and be ready to work tomorrow," he says. "Early. I mean zero dark thirty. Jiji will be saving all her poop for you."

Marcus winks and I shuffle away from him, heading back toward my room. But instead of stopping there, I fix my shoes, run my fingers through my hair to smooth it down, and continue on to the library.

Jennie meets me out front and is already out of breath.

"What's wrong?" I ask.

She tugs on the hem of her hoodie. Except it doesn't say "University of New Mexico" like always. It says "Arizona Polytechnic College."

"I have no idea what school this is. No one in my family ever went there or taught there. I don't even know where it is!" she says, her eyes darting from the hoodie to me. "What happened to all my dad's hoodies? They're all like this."

My stomach twists and my hands start to shake. This is just like the cows that disappeared, the Gearhart brothers' unflavored food, and all the other odd occurrences creeping up at the ranch.

"I'm not sure, but I think it might have to do with all the other things we're trying to figure out. With Bartlett Arnoldson." I bite the inside of my mouth, an idea forming in my brain. "Do you think he's somehow changing everything on the ranch so people won't like it here anymore and will leave? So he'll get his land back?"

"I mean, I guess it's possible. He definitely didn't want anyone new arriving. Maybe that's why he's been targeting you. So we'd better get going. I don't know how long I can hide my messed-up clothes from Mom," Jennie says, her voice shaking. She hands me a hiking pack she prepared. I sling the green nylon bag over my shoulders, and we start down the path toward the Cauldron Mesa trailhead.

Touching my thumb to each of my fingers over

and over, I try to calm my nerves. Jennie and I walk past a group of paleontologists arguing next to the library.

"You were supposed to bring the chisels and brushes!" a red-haired woman says, holding out a canvas bag.

"I did! I don't know what happened!" a short man replies, his hands on his hips.

The woman shakes the bag in the man's face. "This is filled with boxes of spaghetti! Do you think this is a joke?"

Jennie raises her eyebrow at me. We round the corner past the dining hall and see a group of painters with easels set up to capture the rock cliffs towering over scraggly bushes and meandering cacti. I spy one artist practically stabbing her canvas with a thick brush and mumbling to herself, "Why does the paint keep disappearing?"

The Bartlett Arnoldson Effect seems to be spreading like a stink bomb in the Hedor Swamps.

"So once we get to the cabin, what're we gonna do?" Jennie asks as we walk past the circle of rocks I saw on our hike my first day on the ranch. Jennie told me it was a prayer labyrinth. I slow down because I'm already out of breath and let my eyes scan the pattern of rocks making a maze in the shape of a circle. There's a large black tree next to the labyrinth that looks like it got struck by lightning. My stomach twists. "Like, if we see Bartlett Arnoldson, the green-sweater-wearing weirdo, what's the plan?"

I bite my lip. "Um, my big plan ended with getting you to come with me."

Jennie chuckles. She starts biting her fingernails as her eyes scan the rocks and cacti around us. "So you really think he's a ghost? That's so awesome. I mean, I might pee my pants, but that's still awesome. We're gonna meet a cow-stealing, serial-killer zombie."

"Zombies are different from ghosts."

"Well, neither are good, right?" Jennie gnaws on her fingernail with increased intensity. She chuckles to herself. "My dad would've thought this was amazing. He would've probably taught us the complete history of ghosts in New Mexico and figured out exactly what this guy was up to. He was, like, the smartest person ever."

Jennie stops biting her nails and drops her hand to

her side. The breeze picks up and blows dirt in our faces. I cough and wave my hand in front of my face.

"My mom would do a despojo on the whole ranch. Like, burn all kinds of herbs and everything," I tell her. "It would get rid of the bad spirits, and probably ghosts and zombies, too."

I dig my thumbnail into the pads of my fingers.

"And, like, if my dad and your mom teamed up, they'd be unstoppable. A ghost-fighting superduo." Jennie's voice catches in her throat. "Or, like, they would've been."

My feet skid to a stop on the narrow trail, kicking small pebbles across the dirt and over the edge. I look down and watch the small rocks sail through the dry air.

My brain tumbles through all the things I should say to Jennie. All the ways I should comfort her and make her feel better.

But I don't know how. Mom is always the one who knows the exact right thing to say. That ability must've skipped a generation with me.

"I was wondering," Jennie says, pulling on the hem of her Not University of New Mexico hoodie. "How'd you and your friends get into your game? Your Oblivious Era game?"

I chuckle, glad Jennie's changed the subject. "The Forgotten Age?"

"Yeah, that."

We're getting closer to the cabin and I need to distract myself, mostly because I have no idea what I'm going to do when I get there and I'm trying to ignore how tired my legs are. So I'm happy to tell Jennie. "When we were in third grade, we always used to trade books we were reading behind our notebooks while our teacher would be at the front of the classroom. We'd tell each other the stories we'd read at recess and see who could top the other two with how outrageous their story was. Then Beto found a Forgotten Age starter kit at the library and told us it was just like the stories we were telling each other. We spent every weekend after that in the library playing The Forgotten Age."

"That sounds amazing. Seriously the best." She wipes her eye with the back of her hand, and I can't decide if it's because of dust or something else.

I nod my head and continue. "The character choices

in the game are thief, warrior, healer, fool, and mage. I feel like you'd be a healer. And your special characteristic is charisma. I think that you once entranced an entire horde of blargmores by telling them a story that left them in tears, letting our traveling party sneak by without notice."

I look at Jennie and wink. "Or you gave them a three-hour-long lecture on the best snacks, and they fell asleep."

Jennie shrugs. "Probably the second one."

We talk about The Forgotten Age as we hike along the trail. We talk about the best way to defeat rabid blargmores as the trail grows steep and our shoes slip in the dirt. We talk about how to avoid getting stuck in the Hedor Swamps as the path cuts between two rock faces. We talk about why you should never accept a drink from an orcling in a tavern as we guzzle from our water bottles, the sun now high in the sky.

We talk about everything except our parents.

My calves ache, my shoulders hurt, and my lungs feel like they're being squeezed by the warty fist of a giant racknoll.

"How much farther?" I ask Jennie as I wheeze.

She pulls the trail map from the back pocket of her shorts. Tracing her finger along the line for the trail, she looks down the path and narrows her eyes.

"It should just be around the corner. Assuming I'm right about how far we've gone. And honestly, of course I'm right. Duh."

My stomach starts to feel like a shaken bottle of soda and I swallow hard, willing myself not to throw up.

As we come around a corner on the trail between two rock faces, the path opens up and reveals a small cabin with a thatched roof that's been built directly into the side of a rocky hill. Small sections of the walls are missing, crumbled pieces on the ground. The roof sags to one side and looks like a strong fart from a passing bird could collapse it.

"Mr. Jonas says this kind of cabin is a jacal. The walls are mostly mud that they stacked between wood poles. Which is why it looks like it was made by kindergartners playing at the beach."

Or two serial killer brothers, I think, but I don't bother to correct Jennie.

"Let's go inside!" Jennie says, grabbing my hand again and dragging me toward the cabin.

I look down at my University of Miami Hurricanes T-shirt with holes in the armpits and my khaki shorts that still have Mia's poop stains on one leg and wonder if this is really the outfit I want to die in.

Jennie and I approach the cabin, and it looks even worse up close. We walk around the sides and front of the cabin since the back connects to the towering rocky hill behind it. I don't dare touch any of the stones in the walls because they could crumble at any moment.

"Well, I guess we have to see if the ghost of Bartlett Arnoldson is inside," Jennie says. Her grip on my hand tightens and I hope she can't notice how much I'm sweating.

"Do we, though?" I groan.

Jennie laughs. "We didn't come all this way for nothing. Like, seriously, why hike four miles just to chicken out in the end? My idea of fun is trying all the flavors of Japanese KitKats. Not shuffling my feet in the dirt."

Jennie and I step cautiously into the cabin, making sure not to brush up against the doorframe in case the slightest bump collapses the front wall. Our eyes take a moment to adjust to the lack of light in the cabin, especially in comparison to the bright sun glaring at us outside. The air inside is considerably cooler, too. So even if this is Bartlett Arnoldson's cursed murder cabin, I wouldn't mind staying here for a while to recover from the hike.

Jennie and I scan the one open room of the cabin. There isn't anything inside except for a few rocks that have crumbled from the walls. The back of the cabin has been dug into the rock hill like a cave. It's completely dark there, hiding anything that could be inside.

"We should check out that part, too," Jennie says, pointing to the cave.

"Again, do we, though?"

Ño, this really is the outfit I'm going to die in. At least I'm wearing clean underwear.

For now.

Jennie walks in front of me, still gripping my hand. I hope she can't tell that it's shaking.

"What's that?" I ask, my eyes continuing to adjust to the darkness.

In the corner of the dug-out room, there's a small circle of rocks. In the center lies a pile of gray ashes, like someone had a fire going. Empty chip bags and crushed plastic water bottles are scattered to the side.

"So since when do ghosts need fires to keep warm and food and water so they don't starve?" Jennie asks, saying out loud exactly what I'm thinking.

I start to answer her, but a shout outside stops me.

Jennie and I didn't see anyone else on the trail out here. I have no idea who, or what, is here with us.

The cries grow louder and I strain to make them out.

"Wait! I have to talk to you!" a muffled voice shouts through the wall.

"Um, Jennie, do you hear that?" I ask, inching away from the main room of the cabin and farther into the cave.

Jennie opens her mouth to answer, but the only sound that comes is a scream.

Her voice echoes on the rocks as the stone walls of the cabin shake and the wooden slats and beams of the roof snap and break.

I push Jennie back into the safety of the cave as the cabin is demolished behind us. Casting a glance toward the tumbling walls, I watch the last rays of light seeping in through the disintegrating walls and see a flash of green.

The man who's been harassing me on the ranch since I arrived stands there, a shocked look on his face as the crumbling cabin seals me and Jennie in darkness.

CHAPTER 12

WHEN BETO, YESI, and I first started playing The Forgotten Age at the library, Yesi always wanted to explore the dungeons in Gloudon Castle. It didn't matter how much Beto told her they were so dark that our eyes would hurt trying to see something. That the air was so musty, we'd choke on the staleness. She still wanted to run down the winding, slippery stone steps because she was certain that somewhere in the depths of the dungeon, a treasure was waiting for her.

She was never right.

I feel like Yesi now, coughing as I lie on the dirt floor of the cave. My ankle pulses with pain, and I realize it's pinned under one of the rocks that trapped me and Jennie.

I feel a tug under my arms, pulling me from the rock.

"I've got you, Rafa," Jennie whispers, her voice shaking. "Just hang on."

I crawl toward her as she pulls. My foot finally frees itself, but sharp pain erupts from my ankle as the rock leaves long scrapes on my skin. I scramble over to Jennie and sit next to her, our backs against the far end of the cave.

With the amount of damage points I've just taken, my player character would be absolutely deceased. My mage would be completely wiped off the board and out of the game.

"What just happened?" she asks, grabbing my arm and clinging to it so hard that she practically cuts off my circulation.

"I'm not sure," I tell her, rubbing my sore ankle. "Something made the whole cabin collapse."

In the dark, I can hear Jennie's quick breathing. "Something or someone?"

The flash of green I saw before the cabin completely eroded sparks across my mind.

"Bartlett?" I mumble.

Jennie's grip on my arm tightens. "What? It was him?"

I nod my head, even though Jennie can't see me. "I saw him. He looked at me right as everything came down. But he looked different than the picture in the book. Yeah, he was wearing the same green sweater, but he was heavier than the guy in the photograph. Maybe shorter, too?"

"Do you still think it was him? Do you think he made it happen?"

I groan, my voice echoing off the crumbled cabin walls. "I don't know anymore. Maybe. Can ghosts change their appearances?"

Jennie shuffles closer to me as we huddle together. "But, Rafa, how would a ghost do something like that? I didn't think they could touch anything."

I think about the unlocked gate in the pasture. The rocks that flew at me when we tried to round up the horses. The note left for Jonas. The books thrown all over the floor in the library. And now the cabin.

All those things require touching something.

So either Bartlett is a very different kind of ghost . . .

Or he's something else altogether.

"Rafa," Jennie whispers. Her voice quivers and echoes on the rock walls. "I'm scared."

"Me too."

Jennie's light chuckle startles me. "So neither of

us is gonna be the 'take charge, save us from certain doom' type?" she asks.

"Not it."

"Not it, either."

We sit in silence. With my hand that isn't clinging to Jennie's arm, I count my fingers. I count them until my nails dig into the pads. I'm certain I've scratched off all my fingerprints.

"Should we try to move the rocks and dig ourselves out?" I ask, trying to ignore the pain in my fingertips.

Jennie grunts. "No. Definitely not. I know at least that much. We might loosen everything and topple even more rocks on top of us. Bad idea."

"Any chance you packed a flashlight in either of our packs?" I ask, trying to banish from my brain the image of Jennie and me buried under heavy stones.

I can feel Jennie shake her head, her braid hitting my shoulder. "Why would we need flashlights for a hike outside in the middle of the day? I'm sorry, Rafa. I'm so sorry. I should've prepared us better for this."

Ño, I've been trying so hard not to get kicked off the ranch, but now I'm never going to get to leave. I'll be stuck in this cabin forever. No more quesitos. No more playing The Forgotten Age. I won't even get to find out if seventh grade is as horrible as last year's seventh graders made it seem.

And Mom. I won't be able to tell her . . .

I stop counting. Moving my hand down Jennie's arm, I grab her hand and squeeze it. Her breathing is heavy and ragged. I can feel her entire body shake every time she exhales.

She's starting to panic. I know because I'm feeling the same way. I'm spiraling down the dungeon steps, picturing us clinging to each other as we run out of air, as spiders, snakes, and earth babies creep out of the darkness and crawl over our bodies.

I need to distract her. I need to distract *myself*. With chatter about how fast alimancitas can run or about the best way to sneak through the Yermola Wasteland without being noticed by orclings.

"My mom has cancer."

I almost don't hear myself say it. The words spill out of my mouth before I can shove them back down my throat. I've never said this out loud before. It's always about how my mom is tired, how she's not feeling well, how she's on a first-name basis with the nurses at the hospital.

But it's never the full truth.

Jennie's breathing stops for a moment and then she lets out one long breath. Her body stops shaking. "Wow. That really sucks," she says, putting her head on my shoulder.

I want to hug her. Most people give me sad eyes and tell me they're sorry, as if they had anything to do with the fact that Mom's body is attacking itself. Or they act like it's no big deal and Mom is some warrior who will beat cancer's butt if she just tries hard enough and wears a lot of pink.

Nobody tells the truth. Which is that it sucks. Plain and simple.

Jennie squeezes my hand again. "Well, your mom is a goddess. How could she not be, giving you those great snacks, right? Mom of the year, if you ask me. We should make her a plaque."

I rest my head on top of hers and feel her shoulders move up and down slowly as she calms down. I close my eyes and focus on the rhythm of our breathing.

"Can I ask you something?" I say, my low voice

echoing in the cave and sounding louder than I want it to.

"You want to know how my dad died, don't you?" Jennie says.

I nod, knowing that Jennie can't see me but can feel me.

She clears her throat. "It was a car accident. So I didn't get to say goodbye."

I squeeze Jennie's hand and don't ask her anything else. I don't prod for details.

She's told me everything she wants to say.

The sharp rock wall we're leaning against makes my back ache, and I squirm. My neck starts to itch, and I try not to think of all the things that might be crawling in the cave that I can't see.

I shift my weight and Jennie lifts her head from my shoulder. I can't tell how much time passes by. My ears strain for any sound outside. Crickets, howling coyotes, other hikers. But it's silent. My legs start to tingle from sitting on the hard floor of the cave.

"Should we at least try?" I ask her. "You know, moving the rocks? We can't stay here forever."

Jennie sighs. "It seems like our two options are to

sit in this cave for the rest of our lives, until two kids fifty years from now find our bones when they go on a hike that every single adult told them not to, or we can move the rocks and risk having them topple down on us."

"And then kids fifty years from now will find our crushed bones when they go on a hike they weren't supposed to do."

Jennie chuckles. "Exactly."

"I'd rock-paper-scissors with you to figure out which we should do, but I can't see your hand," I say, crouching on the ground as the dirt floor digs into my knees.

"I pick rock."

"That's not how the game works."

Jennie sighs. I think she tries to hit me in the arm but she misses, because all I feel is a whiff of air. "I mean let's move the rocks, genius."

Jennie and I crawl toward the cave opening, feeling along the walls until the solid rock gives way to broken-up pieces.

"Is it better to pull rocks from the middle or pick a side?" I ask.

I hear Jennie exhale quickly. "My guess is from one of the sides. I think it'll be more stable that way. But I'm just talking out of my butt here. I have no idea what we're doing."

"Me neither. So let's get started, I guess."

Jennie and I work slowly, bumping into each other a lot as we feel the rocks in front of us and try to pull the loose ones and move them to the back of the cave. We start at the top and lug the rocks one by one. Our progress is slow. Soon, our breathing is heavy and loud.

I feel like we've been hauling rocks for hours but the cave hasn't gotten any brighter.

"Rafa, not to be all negative, but is this really going to work? I still can't see anything and I lost all feeling in my fingers a while back. Like, I'm pretty sure I still have all ten of them, but who knows at this point?"

"I've hit my legs on the rocks so much that I think my kneecaps poked right out of my skin an hour ago. So I guess no more wearing shorts for me. Pants the rest of my life," I tell Jennie. Her laugh bounces off the cave walls and wraps around me.

"Breaking news—fingerless, knee-less children

found in cave," Jennie says, lowering her voice like the most serious newscaster. She bumps into me with a rock cradled in her arms.

"Mistaken for bloodthirsty zombies as they crawled out of the cave, the boy and girl were immediately put down by the authorities who had surrounded them on horseback," I add, my back straining as I pull another rock to the back of the cave.

Jennie stumbles into me and laughs. "Vultures circled their bodies for three hours before snacking on their eyeballs. Deciding the boy and girl actually didn't taste very good, the vultures flew off in search of green chili burritos."

The cackle that erupts from my throat makes me double over. Jennie and I hold on to each other, our laughter filling the cave as tears fall from our eyes.

"Alvarez! Is that you in there?"

I stand up straight and shake my head, unsure if my exhaustion is making me hear things.

"Did you hear that?" I ask Jennie. She's still holding on to my arm, laughing.

"Alvarez! Man, if you're in there, shout or something so we can hear you," the voice says again. Even though the sound is muffled, I know it's Marcus because he's the only one on the ranch who calls me by my last name.

"Marcus? Is that you?" I shout as loudly as I can. I reach for Jennie's hand and grab it as my heart pounds.

"Yeah, man. It's me. You all right?" Marcus says.

"Is Jennie there, Rafa? Is she okay?" another voice says.

Jennie gasps. "Mom? I'm here!" she shouts.

"Back up, Alvarez. We're gonna dig you both out," Marcus tells us.

My heart jumps into my throat. "We've been working on the right side," I tell him. "The rocks should be thinner there."

Jennie and I stand back, clinging to each other. Jennie's nails dig into my arms as my chest heaves.

Eventually, dim evening sunlight peeks through a gap as a rock tumbles from the top of the cave. More rocks give way, and Jennie and I squint as light seeps in.

My stomach flip-flops when Marcus's face pops into the space that's been created in the rocks. His eyes are wide and his lips are in a tight line.

"Hang on," he says, his voice shaking.

The space grows bigger as more and more light spreads into the cave. Jennie and I watch Marcus and Ms. Kim move rocks away. I stand on my toes and see that they're passing them to Jonas.

Eventually, the opening is big enough to crawl through. I squat down and Jennie stands on my bent leg, crawling over the rocks. Marcus lifts and pulls her through the space.

"Gimme your hand, Alvarez," Marcus says, reaching through the opening.

I grasp Marcus's hand, and he pulls me through as if I weigh as little as an underfed alimancita.

Jennie is hugging her mom and apologizing over and over while Jonas looks at me and wipes his glasses on the edge of his shirt.

Before I can say anything, Marcus grabs me. His lips are tight and his jaw flexes as he grips my arms. He pulls on my clothes, lifts my arms, turns my head in his big hands, inspecting me for injuries with a panic that flames his eyes.

"Olstead, you okay? Not hurt? Tell . . . tell me you're okay, Olstead," he stammers.

I nod but say, "Marcus, I'm Alvarez. My name's not Olstead."

"You can't do that, Olstead. You can't do that to me," he says, his breathing heavy.

Jennie's mom looks from me to Marcus. She places a light hand on his shoulder and squeezes. Marcus releases my arms and shakes his head.

"We didn't know where you were," Ms. Kim says. "Marcus went to your room to see how you were feeling, but you weren't there. So he came to the library to ask Jennie if she'd seen you. That's when we figured out the story you'd made up. It wasn't until one of the visitors said he saw you both near the Cauldron Mesa cabin that we found you."

Ms. Kim brushes Jennie's hair out of her face as Jennie clings to her, still apologizing over and over as tears slide down her cheeks.

"I don't even want to think about what could've happened if we hadn't looked here. Thank goodness someone told us where you were," Ms. Kim says.

Marcus finally lets go of me but keeps clenching his fists. He closes his eyes and takes a deep breath.

I swallow hard and shake my head.

"We're sorry. This was just one big babosan bomb," I manage to say. "I'm glad you found us."

Jonas clears his throat. "Rafa, I think we'll forget to tell your dad about this. No need to make him worry. You guys are okay now, thanks to an observant visitor."

Jennie lifts her head from her mom's shoulder. "Who told you about us?"

Ms. Kim shrugs. "Just another hiker who was out here. Maybe you passed him. He was wearing brown pants and a green shirt."

Jennie looks at me with wide eyes and I double over, putting my hands on my knees.

Why would the ghost of Bartlett Arnoldson try to save us after making the cabin fall down on us in the first place?

Unless that's not who we've been dealing with all along.

CHAPTER 13

ONCE EVERYONE GOT over their relief that Jennie and I were okay, and we got the all clear from the ranch medic, who said we were physically fine aside from scabbed knees and hands, Jonas, Ms. Kim, and Marcus joined forces to plot our punishment. Jennie and I were banned from pretty much everywhere on the ranch except the barn, the library, the dining hall, and probably the bathroom. And we were *not* allowed to hang out together.

I guess they thought our combined power was too destructive for Rancho Espanto to handle.

Or they figured it was easier to keep an eye on us with me in the barn and Jennie at the library.

But we still had a mystery to solve.

Jennie and I figured out the perfect way to communicate, even with us so far apart. We tape notes to each other on the back of the book drop box outside of the library. I drop off mine in the morning when I'm on my way to the dining hall to stuff my mouth full of unspicy green chili scrambled eggs (all as the Gearhart brothers look at me and scowl). I pick up Jennie's reply when I'm coming back from dinner in the dining hall, after I wolf down the Gearhart brothers' chili burritos.

Rafa, I read this story about a family that thought their house was being haunted but it turned out someone was just living in their attic. Do you think the green sweater man could be someone like that? Also, jjajangmyeon is better than that picadillo you were telling me about.

Jennie, Beto and I once read a story about a ghost that could concentrate all his anger and rage so that he could actually touch things. Maybe Bartlett Arnoldson is doing that? And I do not tolerate slander of any kind against picadillo. Especially if someone says you're supposed to add chorizo to it. That's just ridiculous.

Rafa, I think we should set a trap for the ghost. Do you have any idea how to trap a ghost? A pit with poles sharpened into spears? A cupcake under a box? A trail of shrimp crackers? No, wait, that would be how someone could catch me. Don't tell anyone. I can't let that information get out.

Jennie, it would be a trail of merenguitos for me. I still can't figure out why Bartlett Arnoldson would nearly kill us and then tell everyone where we were so that they could save us. Do ghosts have multiple personalities? Why is he trying to get me kicked off the ranch one day and then saving me the next? He's the most annoying ghost I've ever met. Not that I've met a ton of ghosts.

Between trading notes with Jennie, I spend the week with Marcus in the barn. He shows me how to clean out caked mud from the horses' hooves with a pick.

I organize all the saddles and saddle pads. I clean all the cobwebs and dust piles that have built up in each horse stall so they're not a fire hazard. I learn new words, like *tack* and *harness*, which I imagine would make Ms. Kim proud.

Marcus keeps an eye on me while I work. We don't talk about my getting trapped in the cabin. We don't talk about him panicking and calling me by the wrong name. I remember Marcus telling me that Olstead was the buddy he used to ride horses with, but I don't know why he'd mistake me for him.

I work by myself twice this week while Marcus goes to therapy in Santa Fe. I do the best I can without his guidance, although I am getting the hang of things.

I'm rolling up leg wraps for the horses when Jennie comes skipping into the barn. "Rafa, how do you say *Friday* in Spanish?" she asks me.

"*Viernes.* And are you supposed to be here?"

Jennie dismisses my question with a wave of her hand. "And how do you say *ice cream*?"

"*Helado,*" I tell her. "Why?"

Jennie rolls her eyes and puts her hands on her hips. "It's ice cream Friday! You're coming with Mom and me for ice cream in Florita. Mom says we've earned it. This shop is the best place ever. Don't be worried that it's in a gas station. It's like the only place in Florita at all. It's still super great."

Marcus comes out of his office and nods at Jennie when he sees her. He tries to continue down the barn aisle, but it's too late. Jennie strikes.

"Oh my gosh, Mr. Marcus, you should come, too! They have so many flavors. I'm working my way through all of them. Last time was rum raisin, which should really be wiped from the face of the earth, so hopefully this week's flavor will be better. Like java chip or something."

A smile creeps onto Marcus's face, and he tries to hide it by pursing his lips. "I think I should just stay here, Kim. I'm better company for horses than people."

Jennie groans. "It's ice cream, Mr. Marcus. Ice cream. Don't you like nice things?"

I turn to Marcus and wink. "Yeah, you know she's not going to let this go until you agree, right?"

Marcus looks at Jennie, who crosses her arms and nods.

He sighs. "Sounds like it's ice cream day."

Jennie walks us to where her mom is waiting next to a small bright blue car. "Mr. Marcus is coming, too!" Jennie yells as we approach Ms. Kim.

I pretend not to notice the smile overtaking Ms. Kim's face, which she tries to cover by looking at the ground.

We squeeze into the car, Marcus filling up the entire front seat, his head brushing the roof. Jennie and I sit in the back. Ms. Kim starts to back the car up, when Jennie suddenly shouts, "Stop!"

I look at her as she stares at me with wide eyes. "You . . . you need to put your seatbelt on," she says, pointing a shaking finger at me.

I pull the seatbelt across me and fasten it, the loud click filling the silent car.

Sitting behind Ms. Kim, I can see Marcus in the front seat, his hands clenched around his legs. Ms. Kim looks at Jennie through the rearview mirror and gives her a soft smile.

"Okay, I think we're ready to go now," she says, pulling out of the ranch and onto the winding road leading to Florita.

Ms. Kim tries to make small talk with Marcus as we

drive, but he mostly gives her one-word answers as he looks out the window. I know he's not trying to be rude. Sometimes you just get wrapped up in your own head.

Guillermo used to do that a lot. When he'd drive me to the hospital to visit Mom, sometimes he wouldn't say a word the entire time. I didn't mind the silence.

I watch Jennie as Ms. Kim's car meanders down a hill and over a creek. She's biting her lip, her hands clenched tight in her lap.

Leaning closer to her, I whisper, "I think I've figured it out."

She shakes her head, coming out of her thoughts. "What do you mean?"

I shrug. "I'm pretty sure I've created the Super Snack List to End All Snack Lists. At the top is plantain chips, then honey twists, then sesame candy and banana puffs. And all the Japanese flavors of KitKats except matcha. At the bottom are shrimp crackers."

Jennie chuckles and relaxes. "Okay, first, don't knock matcha or I'll throw you out the window. And second, you can't put something you've never tried at the bottom of the list. That's just stupid. Like, I've never had those guava pastelitos that you're always going on and on about like they're made out of precious baby farts and magic, but I wouldn't put them last."

As we continue on, I stare out the window. This is the first time I've been off the ranch since I arrived two weeks ago. I crane my neck to look up at the towering rock cliffs we pass.

Jennie whispers in my ear, "We're like a traveling band of warriors, in search of sustenance, right?"

I nod. "We're traversing the Orosanto Mountains to reach safety in the Land of the Little Flowers. We just have to make sure we don't encounter any time-warping alosynths."

"But if we do, we'll defeat them with our enchanting words that make them see things," Jennie adds, wiggling her fingers in the air.

For a moment I'm transported back to Miami, with Beto and Yesi at my dining room table as Beto leads us on perilous journeys and Yesi makes all the daring decisions. Mom would always show up at just the right moment to give us quesitos, chips, or tall glasses of Jupiña, before Beto took over snack duty when she got too tired.

We continue our adventure as Ms. Kim pulls into the gas station in Florita. Jennie was right. It really is the only thing in town, which consists of three run-down houses and a lavender field with a guard donkey. The gas station is busy, unlike the rest of Florita. Hikers, road trippers, and scientists and artists headed to Rancho Espanto enjoy one last bit of cell service.

Jennie grabs my hand as we get out of the car. "C'mon, Rafa. I'm starving. I might even try two flavors today."

Ms. Kim and Marcus trail behind us. The inside of the gas station is just what you'd expect, selling snacks and sodas, but it also has hiking and camping supplies and a few groceries. Jennie leads me to the back of the store, where a long freezer case holds at least thirty flavors of ice cream. She scans the flavors and stops in front of one.

"Rum raisin. Definitely not that one," she declares. "Let's see what's next. Bubblegum. That should be good, right?"

I nod. "That's Yesi's favorite. Especially if you mix it with the cotton candy flavor."

Jennie gasps. "Oh my gosh, I have to try that."

Jennie places her order and I get peanut butter ribbon crunch, Ms. Kim gets strawberry swirl, and Marcus gets vanilla.

We walk out to a picnic table next to the station and sit down, while Jennie berates Marcus for his safe choice in ice cream flavors.

"I've had enough adventure in my life, Kim," he tells her. "I'm fine with boring ice cream."

Ms. Kim gives him a sympathetic smile and we dive into our treats. The wind blows through the trees around us, and I can hear the creek behind the station running over rocks.

"So what were you two talking about when we were driving over?" Ms. Kim asks. "I swear I heard something about vanquishing enemies."

Jennie winks at her mom. "It's Rafa's game, The Forgotten Age. A totally amazing role-playing game where you get to be wizards or warriors or super-cool creatures. Remember when he asked you about saving that animal stuck in the tree? That was a scenario from The Forgotten Age."

Ms. Kim's answer was exactly what I'd expect from the world's greatest librarian. She'd look up the best way to save an alimancita and then just do that.

I lick my ice cream, the cold sweetness chilling my tongue. "You'd actually like the game," I tell Ms. Kim. "Books have superpowers in it."

Ms. Kim raises an eyebrow and Marcus chuckles. "I'm listening," she says with a smirk.

"So each character in the game picks a book that has special powers. Like mine downloads your memories. When something happens, it's automatically recorded in the book."

I started off wanting it to remember all of my adventures with Beto and Yesi because I kept forgetting where we were on our journeys. And it would've been nice if it could've recorded everything my English teacher always droned on about as my eyelids drooped. But now I think I'd make sure the book described what Mom's long brown hair looked like when she would flip it over her shoulder. Or how it sounded when she sang along to the radio as we drove to the library.

"Everything?" Jennie asks. "Like, today Rafa went to the bathroom and it was super stinky. No one went in there for the next three days."

Marcus laughs so hard that vanilla ice cream dribbles down his chin.

Ms. Kim passes him a napkin and says, "I'm not related to her."

Jennie rolls her eyes. She takes a massive bite of bubblegum ice cream and I wait for the brain freeze to hit. But she just powers through. "I know exactly what my book would be. So whatever I drew in the book would actually come to life. Like if I drew Choco Pies . . . bam! Choco Pies right in front of me. A whole mountain of them."

I nudge her with my elbow. "That is definitely a brilliant idea."

"I know, right? Just think of the possibilities. I mean, you could even draw people." Jennie stops abruptly, her spoon in midair above her cup, bright blue and pink drips swirling together to make purple. She opens her mouth to speak again but takes a massive bite of ice cream instead.

I know exactly who she is thinking about drawing. I've seen his picture next to Ms. Kim's computer.

Ms. Kim clears her throat. "I think I know what my book would do. It would make all other books completely immune to the elements. That way they can't be damaged."

I nod, still watching Jennie out of the corner of my eye as she concentrates on her ice cream. "That would probably be useful for you, wouldn't it?"

Ms. Kim laughs. "Oh my gosh, it would. I've had returned books that were dropped in creeks, thrown over rock cliffs, covered in green chili stew. I even had one that was bitten by a snake. Two big holes right through the cover."

Marcus licks ice cream off his spoon and I look at him expectantly. "Oh, I have to do this, too?" he asks.

"Of course you do. Be a team player, Coleman," I say, winking at him.

Marcus chuckles. He glances over at Jennie, who still won't look at any of us as she takes her spoon and swirls her ice cream in her cup with it.

"I think my book would be strong enough to repel arrows and swords. Or whatever weapons you have in that game of yours. But the best part would be that it could revive your teammates. All you have to do is smack them across the face with it."

With that, Marcus reaches across the table and taps Jennie lightly on the cheek with his hand. "Pow. You're revived," he says.

A smile creeps across her face and she laughs. Taking her cup and drinking all the melted ice cream, she wipes her mouth with the back of her hand. "I wanna see you running around smacking people in the face with a huge book, Mr. Marcus."

We laugh and finish our ice cream, the sun lowering behind the rock cliffs around us. As Ms. Kim drives us back to the ranch, we keep chatting about The Forgotten Age, about fantasy worlds, about what-ifs.

When we tumble out of Ms. Kim's car back at Rancho Espanto, I shuffle to my room, still floating on the laughter that pushed us along the road.

It's not until I wander into my bathroom to brush my teeth while avoiding Señor Spider that I see it.

Scrawled in red on the mirror above the sink, large angry letters yell at me.

Go home. You shouldn't be here. You're missing too much.

CHAPTER 14

WHEN I WAS in first grade, I was afraid to ride the bus to school. The chance was too high that the driver was secretly an alien who was planning to rocket the bright yellow capsule full of unsuspecting children directly into his spaceship. And even if the driver wasn't an extraterrestrial, what if no one wanted to sit next to me? What if I got motion sickness and threw up my breakfast all over the kid in front of me? I could practically see the bits of half-digested toast in her hair.

The possibilities for absolute disaster were endless.

After I'd left bright red welts on my fingertips from nervously counting my fingers over and over, Mom sat me down in front of a huge plate of quesitos. She rubbed my back as I chewed, bits of pastry plastered on my lips. She made me picture myself driving the bus, steering it away from the hovering spaceship waiting to rocket kids into the atmosphere. She helped me find just the right picture books to keep in my back-pack to occupy me, regardless of who was or wasn't sitting next to me. She taught me how to close my eyes and take deep breaths so I wouldn't blast my breakfast in anyone's face.

But Mom's not here.

And these days, I'm the one who has to rub her back and tell her to imagine things getting better.

So last night I pushed the nightstand in front of my door, the scraping legs echoing in my bare room. I tried to enlist Señor Spider to be my bodyguard but he just looked at me with his eight eyes and crept toward the bathroom, preparing to hide in the folds of my towel.

Someone came into my room while we were in Florita and wrote on my bathroom mirror. Jonas seems fine with me being on the ranch as long as I don't screw anything up, the Gearhart brothers are more concerned with fixing their unspicy food so they can burn a hole in my esophagus again, and none of the painters or paleontologists pay any attention to me anyway.

That only leaves one other person. The man in the green sweater, who I'm beginning to suspect *isn't* the ghost of Bartlett Arnoldson. Maybe he's not a ghost at all.

And if he isn't a ghost, that means he can't pass directly through my closed door. So whatever he is, I'm hoping he's the type of being who will be stopped by a nightstand that will knock him in the shins.

I rub my face and slap my cheeks, trying to wake myself up after a night of wondering if the coyotes howling outside my window were really the green-sweatered man transforming into a blargmore, ready to dine on my small intestine.

Pulling my twenty-sided die from under my pillow, I tell it, "My plan is to defeat the man in the green sweater with carefully placed furniture and a reluctant spider army."

I roll the die and it lands on one.

Before the groan can come up from my stomach and out of my mouth, a loud banging echoes from my door and I jump.

Getting up from my bed, I lean over the nightstand and put my hand on the door. "Who . . . who is it?" I stammer.

"Open up, Alvarez."

I sigh in relief and shove my nightstand away from the door.

"I need your help with something," Marcus says, before I even get it completely open.

"What's wrong?" I ask, taking in Marcus's scrunched eyebrows and tight lips.

He rubs the back of his neck. "I just . . . I need you to check something for me. I need to make sure . . ."

Marcus doesn't say anything else. He just stares at me, but I feel like he's looking right through me.

Shoving my feet in my shoes, I follow Marcus to the barn, the cool morning air swirling around us. I scan the ranch, over rocks and cacti, looking for the man in the green sweater.

Thankfully, he's nowhere in sight.

Marcus and I enter the barn and he stops in front of a stall.

"I need you to look at Frankie," Marcus says. He's clenching and unclenching his fists.

I look in the stall. "That's not Frankie. This horse is brown. Frankie is gray with lots of spots."

Marcus's shoulders relax. "So we agree that this horse is brown?"

I nod slowly and raise my eyebrow. Marcus shakes his hands out at his side.

"I needed to make sure. Sometimes I see things. My brain tricks me," Marcus says, shaking his head.

"Okay, so this horse is actually brown. But do you really think it's Frankie? It's not just another horse that accidentally got moved to this stall?" I ask, examining its dark brown coat. It huffs and drags its hoof across the floor in protest.

Marcus narrows his eyes at the horse. "I thought that, too, at first. But his markings are still the same. He still has the same blaze on his face and socks that are just on his front feet."

I learned my first day in the barn that a blaze is a mark down a horse's nose. It doesn't mean that their face is on fire. And they don't wear socks, either. Those are white markings on their legs that *look* like socks.

"This is definitely Frankie. I'd know that horse anywhere. He nipped my left shoulder like Frankie always does and scratched his hoof on the stall floor three times to say hello. He's the only horse that does that. But what happened to him?" Marcus looks over

Frankie standing in the stall, completely unbothered that his coat morphed into another color overnight.

Disappearing cows. Suddenly unspicy food. Paintings changing appearance. Hoodies switching schools. A horse coat turning colors. And an increasing number of weird things that are popping up at the ranch.

Whoever the man I keep seeing is, I can't help but think he's been causing all these strange things since the day I arrived on the ranch. I just don't know how.

Marcus takes deep breaths in front of me and rubs his eyes. He seems only slightly relieved that we're both seeing the same thing.

"Does that happen a lot?" I ask him. "Seeing things different from how they really are?"

I think about Marcus calling me Olstead after he pulled me out of the collapsed cabin.

Marcus sits down on a hay bale next to the wall and rubs the back of his neck. "Not as much as it used to. But sometimes. Going to therapy really helps."

I sit down next to him. "Guillermo once thought there were people sneaking around outside his house. He came busting into Beto's room when I was staying over, shouting at us to stay down and then yelling at his dad to call the police. But when Beto's dad walked around outside to look, there was no one there."

Marcus rubs his hands on his jeans. "Sometimes our own brains can be our worst enemy."

I want to tell him that my brain usually thinks the worst is going to happen. That a horse is going to kick me in the head. That my teachers next year in seventh grade are going to hang me upside down in the middle of the classroom and use me as a piñata. That Beto and Yesi are going to decide I'm the worst Forgotten Age player and banish me from our group. That Mom—

"Back to work, I guess," Marcus says, running his hand over his hair.

"We're just gonna leave Frankie like that?" I ask, glancing again at the brown horse in the stall.

Marcus shakes his head and rubs his eyes. "I've got no clue how he got that way. So I think our best course of action is wait and see. And we've got a trail ride to get ready for."

"Will Frankie go on it?"

"Probably not a good idea. I don't need him sprouting wings while some poor scientist rides him out to their dig site." Marcus squeezes his eyes shut. "I can't believe I just said that."

"Well, let's get the other horses ready before anything else happens, yeah?" I say, slapping Marcus on the back.

But preparing the horses for the trail ride ends up being as easy as marching through the Yermola Wasteland without an orcling potion.

Marcus explains that we have to groom the horses perfectly because any bits of hay, dried sweat, or shavings from their stall can rub a blister on their backs or bellies when they're wearing a saddle and saddle pad. I brush down Mia carefully, but every time I think I have her coat completely clean, bits of hay and dirt pop up, as if time rewound itself and she's just come out of her stall.

Wondering what in the babosan bomb is going on, I look at Marcus as he grooms Jiji, his teeth biting into his lower lip as he narrows his eyes. I suspect he's having the same trouble.

Grabbing two different curry brushes from the tack room, I hand one to Marcus and shrug.

"This is taking longer than I thought it would," he says.

My arm aches as I reach across Mia's back and drag the curry brush across her hair. When she finally stays clean, I get the fly spray from the tack room and spray down her entire coat before I put her saddle pad and saddle on. As I tighten her saddle around her belly, I notice that I put the prong of her saddle strap two holes tighter than usual. It's like Mia has shrunk before my eyes.

I wonder if I should say anything to Marcus, but then I see that he's having the same problem with Wattson, except Wattson's saddle fits three notches bigger—and he looks like he's grown taller.

By the time we get all the horses clean, sprayed down with fly spray, and settled in their saddles, Marcus and I are breathing hard.

"It's usually not this difficult," Marcus says. He's clenching his fists again and looks at me as sweat drips down his forehead. "What's going on, Alvarez?"

I shake my head. I wonder how much I should tell him. I wonder if he would believe me. But now it seems like things going wrong on the ranch aren't just making things more difficult for me. Marcus and everyone else on the ranch have gotten wrapped up in this mess, too.

"I'm not sure," I tell him. "But I think I can figure it out, okay? I'll make it better."

Marcus swallows hard and sits down on a hay bale. "As long as you and I are seeing the same things, I think I can handle that. When it's just me and my brain . . ."

He puts his head in his hands and takes a deep breath. I sit down next to him and we listen to the horses huffing as they scratch in the dirt with their hooves. The breeze blows through the barn and cools our sweaty backs.

I open my mouth to say something, to reassure Marcus that I won't let him think his brain is sabotaging him. But before I can say anything, he sits up and rolls his shoulders.

"Olstead was my best friend. We enlisted together. Got sent overseas by idiots who don't know a bullet from bologna. We were patrolling together, and one minute he was telling me how he was gonna open his own mechanic shop when we got home and the next minute he was buried under a pile of rock from an explosion. That's it. He was gone."

He's digging his fingers into the fabric of his pants

so hard that I think his veins might pop out of his forearms, the scars on his elbows pulsing.

"I came out here because I kept seeing him everywhere. I'd ride around Houston, go to all the places we used to hang out, and they just seemed empty. All I could think about was that he should be there with me. When you got stuck in that cabin, it reminded me too much of him."

Marcus finally looks at me and I can see tears pooled in his eyes. "I'm sorry I scared you," he says.

I put my hand on Marcus's shoulder. "You didn't scare me. I was so happy to be out of that cabin, you could've called me Mildred or Gertrude or Blanche and I would've been fine with it. You're always okay by me."

I stand up and brush the dirt off my pants. Marcus looks up at me and says, "Well, Mildred, why don't you get going and figure out what's happening here, so we can get back to our regular routine of enjoying coffee and avoiding Jiji's explosive farts."

I chuckle. "Seriously, all these things changing on the ranch and your coffee *still* tastes like toilet water?"

Marcus slaps me on the leg with his gloves and I jog

out of the barn. I head toward the library to fill Jennie in on the weirdness of the morning.

But when I get there, I realize it wasn't just the horses that got affected. The weirdness has oozed across the ranch like the stench in the Hedor Swamps.

The second I walk in the library door, Jennie grabs my arm and pulls me into her mom's office. And then she proceeds to drown me in words.

"Oh my gosh, Rafa. What is going on? Half the books in the library are in Portuguese all of a sudden. I'm all for learning new languages, and you know my mom definitely is, but this is ridiculous. And we had a scientist in here earlier swear he saw a Coelophysis running around. Not a fossil made of bones. Like, the actual dinosaur. Jonas threatened to kick him off the ranch."

Jennie takes a deep breath and lets go of my arm.

"There's also this."

She reaches in a drawer on her mom's desk and pulls out the frame that's usually propped next to the computer. The one with the picture of Jennie, her mom, and her dad. Jennie hands the frame to me and I look at the photograph. It's the picture I expect to see of

Jennie leaning into the Grand Canyon as her dad holds on to her.

Except her dad isn't her dad.

The man holding on to her shirt is white and about twenty years older than Jennie's dad.

Jennie's bottom lip quivers and she clears her throat.

"Who is this?" she asks.

CHAPTER 15

MOM HAS PHOTO albums that line one of the walls of her studio. She takes pictures of leaves, flowers, trees, and anything else that might inspire her metal sculptures. I looked in her albums one day and saw a picture of me as a toddler sitting on the beach at Key Biscayne, trying to eat a fistful of sand. Tucked in between photos of egrets was a one of me trying to ride my skateboard without smashing into our mailbox.

Lately, she's been taking lots of pictures of me on her cell phone. When I'm half asleep eating a peanut butter sandwich before school, she'll snap a quick photo if she's awake. When Beto, Yesi, and I are deep in The Forgotten Age, she'll take our picture as we argue over whether we should try to go around the invading blargmores or attack them head-on.

I often catch her scrolling through them as she lies

in bed. If those pictures, those memories, faded, I don't know if she'd be able to handle that.

And now Jennie's preserved memories of her dad are starting to change.

We know we aren't done with our research. At least this time, it won't involve us hiking four miles to an abandoned, unstable cabin that will try to devour us.

"It's the prayer labyrinth," Jennie whispers to me as we walk to the barn early the next morning. She rubs her eyes and yawns. She probably slept as much as I did last night.

Which is not a lot.

"You mean that storm the day I arrived?" I ask, showing Jennie how much a flake of hay is when we get to the barn.

Jennie dumps the hay gathered in her arms in Frankie's feeder. He's still the wrong color.

"Well, yeah. Everybody on the ranch is talking about it. Because after that, the weird things started. Sure, it rained, but there was a ton of lightning right near the prayer labyrinth. Thunder that made me think my eardrums were going to explode . . . and then nothing. It was over. There was that tree that turned all black from

187

a lightning strike, but that was it. I heard this painter last night at dinner swear that the storm brought bad spirits to the ranch. One of the paleontologists actually agreed with him."

I grab a shovel as Jennie continues feeding the horses and start scooping poop out of Mia's stall.

"Am I getting a two-for-one deal today?" Marcus says, coming out of his office.

Jennie finishes dumping hay in Jiji's feeder and brushes her hands on her jeans.

"Mr. Marcus, I'm helping out Rafa because we have to go figure out what's causing all this weird stuff on the ranch. You know, the 'why the heck aren't my green chili enchiladas burning a hole in my throat' stuff. Because I'm pretty certain I'm gonna kiss an earth baby right on the mouth if anything else happens."

Jennie slides her hands into the pocket of her only UNM hoodie that hasn't changed, and I know that's where she's keeping the picture of herself, her mom, and her not-dad.

I empty the last of Mia's poop into a wheelbarrow and set the shovel against the wall. "We didn't want to leave you with all the work. And I didn't want to lie to you again about what I was really doing. That didn't exactly work out for me last time."

"No worries, Alvarez." Marcus shrugs. "I know all about feeding your supervisors a line. There's a chance I told my CO it took two hours for PMCS so I wouldn't have to do anything else for a while. Sat inside the Humvee out of sight and read a book instead of checking the oil."

Jennie smiles. "Wow, you just said a lot of letters. That's brilliant. I have to remember that. Not that I change the oil on cars or anything. But, like, I bet I could convince Mom it took a superlong time to reshelve the poetry section of the library."

She leans over to me and whispers, "There are strawberry Pocky sticks behind the Joy Harjo books."

Marcus chuckles and takes the shovel from the wall. "Well, go ahead and get out of here. I'll finish up. I think your top priority should be solving . . . that."

He gestures toward Frankie and sighs.

Jennie gives him a thumbs-up. "We got it, Mr. Marcus. You don't need to worry."

I look at Marcus and give him a sympathetic smile. He nods and heads toward Ike's stall.

Jennie grabs my hand and we jog past the library and dining hall and toward the edge of the ranch. The trail curves around cacti and overgrown bushes, but the cacti have purple blossoms instead of yellow and the leaves have fallen off most of the bushes even though it's not winter.

My stomach starts to rumble and I count my fingers. *One, two, three, four. One, two, three, four.*

What if we never figure this out? What if even more things change? Ño, what if Jennie, Marcus, or Ms. Kim turns into a slobbering orcling or toothy blargmore?

"What in the babosan bomb is a prayer labyrinth?" I ask Jennie, trying to distract myself.

Jennie's hands are still shoved in the pocket of her hoodie. "Mom says it's a combination of a circle and a spiral. The one at the ranch is made out of stones placed on the ground. You walk along the space laid out by the rocks to the center of the circle and then it takes you back out again. You can pray or meditate as you walk. You can think about everything or nothing."

We round a corner and Jennie points in front of us. "See?" she says.

Down the hill is a large circle outlined by rocks

next to the tall blackened tree that I spotted when Jennie and I disastrously hiked the Cauldron Mesa trail. The inside looks like a maze bordered by rocks with a smaller circle in the center. It seems like you're supposed to meander the winding path between the stones to reach the center. I'd probably get dizzy, fall down, and hit my head on a rock.

"The rocks look weird, though," she says, walking down the hill. "They're in a different pattern than usual."

My stomach starts to flip-flop and I wrap my arms around my waist, trying to calm myself down. Jennie and I head toward the prayer labyrinth, and I look around for anything else that might be out of place.

Or any*one*.

One, two, three, four. One, two, three, four.

I walk around the outside of the labyrinth, unsure of what I'm looking for. "Did you ever come here much before today?" I ask Jennie. She's walking through the maze, one foot directly in front of the other, her gaze trained on the ground in front of her.

Jennie shrugs. "Right after we moved here, I did. I walked around and around the maze. Every time I took a step, I wished for my dad to be back." She looks up at me. "It obviously didn't work."

My stomach flip-flops again, over and over. I don't know why. I hunch over and wrap my arms tighter around my waist. My ears start to ring, a high-pitched sound like a fire alarm going off. I squeeze my eyes shut.

One two three four one two three four one two three four—

I feel a tug at my arm.

"Rafa, he's here," Jennie whispers, pulling me behind a bush next to the blackened tree.

Jennie and I watch as the man in the green sweater shuffles to the prayer labyrinth. He scuffs his feet in the dirt, sending small dust clouds behind him. He has a rectangular metal box tucked under his arm that glints when the sun catches it. My ears keep ringing. I grab Jennie's hand.

"I guess this is our chance to figure out if he's a ghost or not," she says. Jennie shakes her hand free from mine and picks up a small stone on the ground.

"What are you doing?"

Jennie shrugs. "If he's really a ghost, this rock should go right through him, right?"

"And if he's not?"

"Then I've probably caused bigger problems."

Before I can stop her, Jennie flings her arm back and launches the rock toward the man in the green sweater. My stomach rumbles and I swallow hard to keep from throwing up. The stone missile sails through the air.

And slams into the man's back, tumbling to the ground.

"Oops," Jennie says.

The man spins around, scanning the edge of the labyrinth until his eyes fall on us.

I stumble backward against Jennie and grab her arm.

"I have to talk to you!!" the man shouts, spit flying from his mouth. "You need to leave, now. You can't stay here!"

The man thunders toward us and I fall backward, landing hard on my tailbone. Jennie crouches behind me, trying to pull me up by the armpits.

"Let's get out of here," she hisses in my ear.

Fists clenched at his side, the man towers above me. His eyes dart from me, to Jennie, to the lightning-struck tree.

"You need to go home! You shouldn't be here. You have to get back before it's too late!" the man screams.

Before I can force a question out of my mouth or push myself off the ground, the man grabs me by the arm, hard.

It's as if I've been hit by a mage's freezing spell. My back locks up and I try to scream, but it gets stuck in the back of my throat. I squeeze my eyes shut and gasp.

A beeping sound fills my ears, growing faster and faster until it becomes one continuous sound. A piercing white light floods my brain, and images I can barely make out swirl behind my eyes. Long black pillars shrink and focus until I see that they're really people. Bursts of color appear, swirling around the people. More flowers than I've ever seen.

"Rafa, wake up!" I hear Jennie as if she's calling to me from across the canyon.

I open my eyes and feel Jennie pulling me up, out of the man's grasp. He's writhing on the ground, his hands twitching at his side.

"We need to get away from him," Jennie says, pulling me by the arm.

We run away from the prayer labyrinth as fast as

our shaking legs will carry us. My feet burn and my back aches.

One two three four one two three four one two three four—

I shake my hands to stop myself from counting.

As we pass the dining hall again, completely out of breath, I realize the man was counting his fingers over and over, too.

Just like me.

CHAPTER 16

JENNIE WANTED ME to stay the night with her and her mom last night. But I just shoved the dresser in front of my door again and made Señor Spider promise to crawl up the nose of anyone who tried to come in. My head pounded all night and my ears rang every time I rolled over in bed.

When I stumble out of my room, I walk without thinking. I stare at the ground and watch my shoes get covered in a layer of dirt as I trudge along the path. When I finally look up, I'm in front of the library instead of the barn.

I push through the door in a trance and rub my eyes.

"Hi, Rafa," Ms. Kim says while sorting through books. She looks up at me and her eyes grow wide. "Oh my, sweetie. Are you okay?"

I shrug and my shoulders ache. "Just tired, I guess.

I was wondering if I could use your computer to video chat with my mom."

Ms. Kim smiles and nods. "Of course. Have at it. And then maybe go to the dining hall and get a gallon of coffee. That might help with your day. I've already had four cups to deal with all these strange books on the shelves. It's getting harder and harder to ignore my daughter's stories, honestly."

She gives me a wink and carries a stack of books to another part of the library, suspiciously eyeing one book written in Portuguese. I walk into her office and sit in front of the computer. The space where Jennie's family picture usually is feels especially empty.

I send the video chat request to Mom's account and wait.

I wonder if she's asleep. I wonder if she's at a doctor's appointment. I wonder . . .

The computer chimes and Mom's face appears on the screen.

Her skin is paler than its usual café con leche color, like someone added too much milk. There are dark circles under her eyes. She's wearing a bright green scarf around her head to cover up her lack of hair. She stopped bothering to draw on her eyebrows with a makeup pencil a while ago.

She's still recovering from the stem cell transplant she had two months ago. Mom explained it to me as the doctors taking out cancer cells from her body, scrubbing them clean, and then putting them back in her bone marrow where they would make more clean cells.

I told her that her doctors sounded like wizards from The Forgotten Age.

But the whole process has left her looking like the wizards cast a transformation spell, too.

"¡Oye, mi Pollito! ¿Cómo anda?" she says. Her voice is soft and shaky, unlike the loud voice that used to fill our entire house, laughing as Beto, Yesi, and I entertained her with our latest escapade.

I cover my mouth with my hand so she won't see my bottom lip quivering. Taking a deep breath, I make sure it won't sound like I'm about to cry when I speak. "It's okay. The ranch isn't bad."

Mom smiles and her chapped lips stretch. "Ay, ño ñoñez. I'm glad it's okay. I was worried about you going all the way out there. But there was no point arguing with your father."

She speaks slowly and takes a few breaths between sentences.

"Did you get the snacks I had him send?"

I nod and smile. Yesterday, Jonas showed up in my room with a big green box of Café La Llave. I wondered why he was giving me a year's supply of coffee until I saw that it was a box with my Miami address on it and the address for Rancho Espanto. When I opened it, all my favorite snacks sat inside—plantain chips, merenguitos, chiviricos, ajonjolis, peanut butter candies, and Twizzlers.

I scratch my cheek with my fingernails, not caring that I'm probably leaving marks on my face. "How . . . how have you been?"

"Bueno, good days and bad days, no? I had a good day yesterday. Drew some sketches for a new sculpture. Today, my stomach feels like a blargman is sitting on it, so I'm just resting."

I chuckle. "Blargmore. And you can get rid of them by casting a transformation spell."

"I'll let my doctor know," Mom says, winking.

"I'm sorry I bothered you. If you were trying to rest, I mean."

Mom shakes her head and takes a deep breath. Her shoulders shake and she winces. Collecting herself, she looks at me. "Ay, Pollito, you're never a bother. You call me whenever you want. Two in the morning, ten o'clock at night, I don't care."

I bite my lip so that it stops quivering and look away from the computer so Mom won't see the tears creeping in the corner of my eyes.

"Okay, I'll call you tomorrow morning at three," I tell her, rubbing my sweaty palms on my pants.

She laughs, but it sounds empty. "Bueno, I have to do the mom thing. Are you drinking water? Eating enough? Making friends?"

I nod. "It's super dry here so I have to drink a lot or I'll never pee again. I'm becoming a connoisseur of peanut butter sandwiches so I don't have to eat anything with green chilies, although that's not a problem lately. The guy I work with in the barn is really cool. He's a veteran like Guillermo. And there's a girl here my age who is letting me teach her about The Forgotten Age. We trade snacks."

Mom's eyelids droop as I'm talking and she winces again when she shifts her weight in her chair.

"But I've got to go now, Mom," I tell her, so that she can get off our call and go back to sleep. "I've got lots of poop to scoop today."

"Te quiero, mi Pollito. Siempre," Mom says and blows me a kiss.

"Love you, too," I say, clicking off the call.

I sit and stare at my reflection on the computer screen, wishing it was still Mom's face I was seeing. Wishing I could cast a healing spell and make everything better.

But I'm a twelve-year-old who got sent across the country as punishment for stealing a slushie machine. And healing spells are only real in games.

I leave the library office and spot Ms. Kim again. She's staring at a book spine and mumbling, "Another one? I don't remember this being in Russian."

I shove my hands in my pockets. "Thanks for letting me use the computer," I tell her.

Ms. Kim pushes the Russian book between two other books on the shelf that look like they're written in Chinese and Greek.

"Of course! I hope everything is okay at home," she says.

I nod because I don't want to bother explaining how not okay things are at home.

"Well, these might help you survive working in the barn today." Ms. Kim reaches into her pocket and pulls out three small dark brown wrappers. She hands them to me and I read the word коріко on the label.

"They're coffee candies. My daughter isn't the only one with good snacks," she says, winking.

"Thanks. These look really good," I tell her. "I'll come back when I need about three hundred more to stay awake."

Ms. Kim laughs as I leave the library and head toward the barn, popping all three candies in my mouth and biting down. A strong coffee flavor fills my mouth and I smile.

Mom would love these.

When I finally get to the barn, Marcus looks me up and down and raises an eyebrow.

"You okay there, Alvarez? You look like you jumped out of a C-130 without a parachute."

I groan as I pick up a shovel. It feels like it weighs 536 pounds.

"I didn't sleep much last night."

Marcus takes the shovel from me. "Does this have anything to do with your investigation yesterday? Because Frankie's coat is still the same. Meaning it's not the color it should be. And I can't be certain, but the longer I look at Jiji, the more I think she's developing stripes. Like a zebra."

My shoulders sag. I can't take anything else going wrong. Before I can explain what happened at the prayer labyrinth, we hear a shout.

"Rafa!"

Jennie runs down the center of the barn. She stops in front of us, her breath blowing her purple bangs off her forehead.

"Oh, hey there, Rafa. How are you doing?" she says, out of breath. Her eyes dart from me to Marcus.

I raise my eyebrow. "Good, I guess. You okay?"

Jennie nods. "Just wanted to see how you were after yesterday. You know, after everything."

Marcus leans over and starts scooping out Mia's stall. "He was about to tell me how your research went at the labyrinth."

I look from Marcus to Jennie. She nods. "Tell him."

Taking a deep breath, I launch into my story of the

man in the green sweater—how I'm certain he let the horses out, wrote that confession letter, and destroyed the library. All to frame me. How he yells at me to go home every time I see him. How I saw him before the cabin collapsed on Jennie and me.

"When we went to the prayer labyrinth to get some answers, he showed up," I continue. "He grabbed my arm and when he did, I saw a bunch of weird things and passed out."

Marcus straightens up suddenly. Veins in his forearm bulge as he clenches the shovel. "He what?"

I lift the sleeve of my black T-shirt to reveal a handprint still on my bicep. I thought it would be a bruise, given how hard the man's fingers wrapped around me, but it looks more like a burn. "He grabbed my arm."

Before I can say anything else, Marcus takes off running out of the barn.

I look at Jennie and she groans. "Oh god, I already ran here."

"Let's go," I tell her, running after Marcus.

He's still in sight as we pass the library, but Marcus runs like he's been possessed by a rabid alimancita, and he's too far ahead of us to see once we pass the dining hall. My shoes start to fill with dirt as we run, small rocks poking my heel. Jennie breathes hard next to me.

But we have to make it to Marcus. If he finds the man in the green sweater, I don't want him hurting Marcus. What if he makes Marcus faint, too?

Jennie and I pass a clump of cacti and reach the prayer labyrinth, our legs aching and our lungs burning. Jennie wipes her forehead with the back of her hand.

"Do you see him? Do you see Marcus? Or . . . anyone else?" she asks.

I scan over the prayer labyrinth. The rocks look different than they did yesterday, arranged to make a completely different maze. The burnt-out tree that was struck by lightning still looks the same, though.

But behind it, I spot two men, one towering over the other, crouched on the ground.

"There," I say, pointing to the tree. "They're right there."

We run down to the labyrinth, crossing the stones and approaching the tree.

Next to the soaring rock wall, I see the man in the green sweater lift his hands up in surrender as Marcus overshadows him with his broad shoulders.

"I'm sorry, I'm sorry," the man mutters over and over.

"You're sorry?" Marcus shouts. "You don't ever lay a hand on him again, you hear me?"

The man lowers his arms. "Ño! He can't stay here. He has to go home."

Jennie grabs my hand when I try to approach them and shakes her head.

Marcus takes the man by the neck of his sweater and lifts him up. "Why do you keep saying that? Who are you?"

The man looks past Marcus with his dark brown eyes and lands on me. His gaze narrows and he sighs.

"My name . . . is Rafael Alvarez."

CHAPTER 17

MY HAND SHAKES as I take my twenty-sided die out of my pocket and flip it on the table in the library.

Marcus, Jennie, and Ms. Kim look at me as the die lands on twenty.

I don't bother telling them I told the die, "I'm going to walk straight into a huge vat of the Gearhart brothers' green chilies because that makes more sense than what's happening now."

The man in the green sweater—Mr. Not Bartlett Arnoldson—whose real name I still can't bring myself to say, stares at me from across the table.

Ms. Kim stands next to me, rubbing her temples. "Run this by me again? What're you talking about?"

Jennie takes a deep breath. "Oh my god, Mom, I already told you. This guy here—"

"No, not you," Ms. Kim says, shaking her head. "Someone else."

I clear my throat as I watch the man scratch the scar above his left eyebrow. The same scar I have. Like me, his shaggy dark hair covers it up, which is probably why I didn't notice it before. That and the fact that I was distracted by him scaring me all the time.

I tell Ms. Kim the story I told Marcus—how Not Bartlett Arnoldson yelled at me whenever I saw him, how he threw rocks to make the horses run at me and probably wrote a fake confession letter that blamed me for it, how he made the cabin on the Cauldron Mesa trail collapse, how I passed out when he grabbed me at the prayer labyrinth.

Ms. Kim narrows her eyes at the man and he squirms under her stare, counting his fingers over and over. I squeeze my hand into a fist when I realize I'm doing the same thing.

"And you said your name is Rafael Alvarez?" Ms. Kim asks.

The man nods, biting his lip.

Ms. Kim looks at me. "So you happen to have the same name. I'd say the odds are low but not impossible for that."

Marcus steps next to me and places a heavy hand

on my shoulder. "I think it's a little more than that," he says. "But I'm not sure."

Jennie crosses her arms and glares at the man. "Why shouldn't we just call the police on you? You've been bothering Rafa the entire time he's been here. You should be kicked off the ranch. People get booted for littering here, and you've done a lot worse."

The man lowers his head and mumbles, "He's the one that needs to be kicked out. He has to go home."

I slam my hand down on the table. My palm stings. "Stop saying that!"

Marcus squeezes my shoulder. "If I were you, man, I'd start explaining myself right now. And no more of this 'he has to go home' nonsense. We need a real explanation."

The man looks up at Marcus and flips his dark brown hair off his forehead. I wince again at the shared habit.

"I'm from the year 2062. I'm him from forty years in the future," the man says, pointing at me.

Jennie coughs. I sink back in my chair, my stomach rolling and my palms sweating. Marcus pulls a chair next to me and sits down.

"I'm gonna need more than that, man," he says. "Because that sounds ridiculous."

The man leans forward, resting his elbows on the table. He takes a deep breath. "My name is Rafael Manolo Alvarez. I was born on July 21, 2010."

He pauses and Jennie looks at me, raising her eyebrow.

I nod. "Yeah, that's my middle name and birthday."

Jennie huffs. "Well, anyone can look that up."

The man continues. "In the future, I'm a particle physicist studying wormholes. My research involves locating, stabilizing, and expanding them. My team initially thought we could extract renewable energy from wormholes. But then I discovered they could be used to travel in time as well."

Jennie looks at me again and I shake my head. "Don't look at me, I got a C minus in science last year."

The man sighs and rubs the corners of his mouth with his fingers. "You . . . I do better later on in school. I was more . . . motivated. I started out at a community college and worked my way up to a doctorate in particle physics. The goal was always to find a way to travel in time. That's all I ever wanted. That's all we wanted."

That doesn't sound like me at all.

"You should ask him something only you would know," Jennie says to me.

I bite my nails, trying to sort through all the thoughts tumbling through my brain and making my ears ring. "I've got it." I narrow my eyes at the man. "What was the first thing I did for Mom after she found out she had cancer?"

Ms. Kim gasps and places her hand on my leg. Marcus stares at me, but I keep my gaze on the man. He'd flinched when I mentioned Mom.

He runs his hands through his hair, his fingers slightly shaking. "You sat next to her bed and gave her your blue twenty-sided die, the one you always thought was good luck. You told her you'd find a way for her to escape the dungeon she was stuck in."

Jennie smiles and winks at me. "That sounds like Rafa."

I nod. "He's right. So, yeah, I think he's telling the truth," I say, swallowing hard to keep myself from throwing up. Hot bile still manages to climb into my throat and I squeeze my eyes shut, concentrating on my breathing and not the fact that I'm sitting across from someone from the future. Anything but that.

Jennie's leg bounces up and down as she drums her fingers on her thighs. I think she might explode any moment.

"So you time-traveled?" she asks, her voice impossibly full of more energy than normal. "Like, you literally zapped yourself from the future to now?"

The man sighs and pulls open a canvas sack labeled GOLDEN MARK BASMATI RICE. He's obviously stolen it from the Gearhart brothers' inventory. But instead of taking out the beginnings of green chili stew, the man sets a rectangular metal box on the table between us.

"If you need more proof, this is it. This is the device I used," he says.

I scan the box and the small knobs and dials on the side. It looks like something I could've made as a science project in the second grade.

Jennie reaches her hand out to touch the device, but the man pulls it back. "It took my team ten years to develop this. Countless trials and errors. One guy almost lost half his arm to 1965."

Marcus lets out a chuckle and then swallows it down, looking at me. "Sorry," he whispers.

Jennie hasn't quit vibrating with excitement. "So you could tell us all about the future, right? Do we finally wise up and get a woman president? Do American grocery stores realize Korean snacks are superior to pretty much everything? Do librarians let you check out as many comics and graphic novels as you want and quit calling them dessert books?"

She stares at the man as if she's looking through his skull. I'm still trying to not throw up.

The man takes a deep breath. "Yes."

Jennie gasps. "Wait. Yes? Which part? Which part is a yes?"

The man shakes his head and waves his hand dismissively. "Now that that's been established, we need to get to what's really important. I know that maybe I've been going about this the wrong way, but you really do need to go back to Miami. You should be with our parents."

I start counting my fingers again. I can't stop myself.

"The wrong way? You almost got me and Jennie killed. Just so you could mess things up and get me sent home?"

The man shrugs. "I didn't mean for that to happen. I was just trying to talk to you so I could explain everything, but then I tripped and slammed into the cabin wall. I didn't know it was so unstable and never meant for you to get trapped. I think we can agree that I don't want something bad happening to you, since it would have disastrous effects for me."

Jennie's eyes grow wide when she realizes what the man is saying. "Oh my gosh, if something had happened to Rafa, you would've just disappeared. Or like if he'd gotten superbad cuts on his knees from the rocks, you'd have scars. Wow, this is like the coolest thing ever."

"No, not cool," I say, and glare at the man. "You've been yelling at me for weeks, coming in my room and leaving notes, making it seem like I was doing all these terrible things on the ranch."

The man hunches over and wrings his hands. "Well, all good scientists change their methods after evaluating their effectiveness. First, I thought I could scare you away, and then I figured I'd try to find a way to get you kicked out. When that didn't work, I tried explaining things to you, but I never got the chance."

Biting my lip, I think about all the strange occurrences at Rancho Espanto. "But how did you make the cows in the canyon disappear, or the Gearhart brothers' food not spicy, or the rocks in the prayer labyrinth and the books in the library change? How did those fit in your plan to make me leave?"

"That's both our faults, I'm afraid," the man responds, running his fingers through his hair again. "You and I shouldn't exist in the same time or place. We're the same person taking up the same timeline. We're matter and antimatter fighting for dominance."

Jennie's mouth drops open as the man talks. She reaches behind a large book of landscape paintings and extracts a bag of Hi-Chew candies. "Um, doesn't it cause universe-ending explosions when those two things collide? I read somewhere that matter and antimatter particles getting together was, like, super-bad. The worst thing ever. Why didn't you blow us all to oblivion when you grabbed Rafa at the prayer labyrinth?"

The man shakes his head. "Right now, we're just warping reality. That's why you're seeing strange things happening around the ranch. But the longer we stay in proximity, the worse it will get."

Marcus crosses his arms. "So when you were talking about Rafa needing to go home, is it because of these universe-altering issues?"

The man bites his lip. He opens his mouth to speak but then closes it, wringing his hands until his knuckles crack. Finally, he says, "Yes. If he doesn't leave, reality will continue to unravel here. The whole situation will devolve. And there's a risk that the changes we're seeing will become permanent the longer we're in the same timeline."

My stomach rolls again. Jennie passes me a mango Hi-Chew, but I push it away. "Why do I have to be the one to leave? Why don't *you* leave? You're the one causing problems in the first place. If you knew it was going to disrupt this timeline, why'd you come here to begin with?"

"You and I are tethered together. I intended to travel back in time to Miami. But you weren't there. You were here. So this is where I showed up," the man explains, counting his fingers again as his eyes dart around the room. "I can't leave until I know you've gone back home. I have to ensure that everything is safe again. The important thing is that you leave the ranch and go back to Miami. To be with your family."

Ms. Kim sits down next to me and puts her hand on my back. "Rafa, I know this is a lot to take in. I'm having a hard time believing it myself. But assuming everything this man is saying is true, don't you think it would be best to go home? I'm sure you'd rather be with your mom right now."

I stand up quickly, kicking my chair out behind me. It crashes to the ground and everyone jumps. "I'm not leaving! I don't want to go home!"

I run out of the library, away from everyone's surprised stares and the man's fists banging on the table. I run toward my room so I can roll my twenty-sided die, telling it I'm going to stay in this fantasy world for as long as I can.

CHAPTER 18

ONE OF THE biggest choices Beto, Yesi, and I made in The Forgotten Age was when we had to decide whether to enter the castle at Eldervorn or go around it and back to our homeland past the Cambimuda Realm. Avoiding the castle would've ended our journey. But I wanted to keep playing. To keep wandering around. So I decided to risk all our lives and explore the castle. Sure, it was selfish, but meandering through the dark and dangerous towers was better than getting up from the dining room table and starting the list of chores Dad had left for me.

I wipe tears from my eyes with the back of my hand. A soft knock on my door startles me.

"Rafa? You there?" Jennie says.

"Yeah," I call. "You can come in."

Jennie shuffles into my room and sits down next to me on my bed. We listen to the coyotes howling outside as the sun sets. Jennie reaches in the pocket of her hoodie and passes me a small bag of banana puffs.

"Native plants book section," she tells me.

I turn the bag over in my hand but don't open it. I'm still breathing deeply, trying not to throw up.

My room gets darker as the sun sets, but we don't bother turning on a lamp. The crickets outside start chirping and I close my eyes, focusing on the rhythm of their noise.

I feel Jennie's fingers wrap around mine, and she squeezes my hand.

"My dad used to take me every Friday to an ICEE stand when we lived in Albuquerque. I'd get a piña colada ICEE and he'd get grape. I'd make fun of how his lips turned purple. He'd tell me about what he was teaching in his classes, about the crazy excuses his students would give for not writing their papers, about all the things he was learning for his own research projects."

Jennie's voice floats in the room, barely a whisper. I keep my eyes closed as tears crawl down my face.

"I'd tell him about how Bryce Collins was teasing

me and my great plan to feed Bryce high-fiber snacks that would keep him in the bathroom all day. I'd tell him about how I was going to read every graphic novel ever written, no matter how long it took me."

My muscles give out and I put my head on Jennie's shoulder. She tightens her grip on my hand.

"Yeah, he was my dad. He'd tell me to brush my teeth, give me 'that look' when I got a bad grade. But he was my friend, too, you know? He would've been someone I'd want to hang out with even if I wasn't related to him."

Jennie clears her throat. I can tell she's crying, too, her tears falling on the top of my head. This is the most she's ever told me about her dad.

"I think you feel that way about your mom, too. Don't you want to see her?"

I take a deep breath, unsure if I'll be able to speak without my words coming out in a choked sob.

"She doesn't look like my mom anymore," I tell Jennie. "She doesn't act like my mom anymore, either."

Jennie squeezes my hand again. "But she's still your mom."

I sit up and open my eyes. Jennie gives me a weak smile and wipes the tears from her cheeks.

I swallow hard. "I don't want to watch her fade away."

Putting my head in my hands, I sob. Jennie lightly pats me on the back.

She lets me sit and cry. She doesn't tell me things will get better. She doesn't tell me I'm a bad person for not wanting to go home. She doesn't tell me I have to be strong. She just lets me cry.

When the sun has completely set, when the crickets have stopped their song, I shed the last tear I can, wipe my nose with the back of my hand, and sit up.

Jennie takes the bag of banana puffs off the bed and opens them. Popping one in her mouth, she chews, her eyebrows knitted together and her mouth in a tight line.

I feel a chuckle bubble from the back of my throat and escape my mouth.

"What's so funny?" Jennie asks.

"Random thought. My mom's favorite band always talks about loving yourself. Love yourself this. Love yourself that."

"So?"

My shoulders shake as I laugh again. "Yeah, I don't love myself. That guy is *really* annoying."

Jennie slaps my arm lightly. "We need a plan. A plan like we're Forgotten Age travelers going up against a time-traveling wizard, right?"

I nod. Jennie holds the banana puff bag out to me, but I shake my head.

"So you want to stay here at the ranch, right?"

I sigh and nod. "I can breathe here. The air is too sad at home," I whisper.

Jennie nudges me with her elbow. "The air smells like horse poop here, but okay, I get it. So we need a plan. Something to get rid of Future You—"

"Please don't call him that," I say, my stomach flip-flopping again.

"Okay. We need a plan to get rid of that person who just happens to be sitting in the library right now while also letting you stay on the ranch."

Jennie and I sit in silence again. I half wish Señor Spider would come crawling out of the bathroom and tell us what our great plan should be. But he's probably just waiting above the showerhead, ready to jump on me like always.

I take my twenty-sided die from my nightstand and roll it between my fingers.

"You know, one time Beto, Yesi, and I were stuck in the Hedor Swamps. A toxic mist was making its way to us and it seemed like there was no escape. And it turns out there wasn't, because in the end, we realized the best choice was to just cast a spell to change where we were."

I take the bag of banana puffs from Jennie and shove three in my mouth.

"I'm gonna pretend I know what you're talking about, Rafa," Jennie says.

"I'm saying that we need to change our reality," I tell her.

"How do we do that?"

"We lie."

I thought I was a good actor. I thought my performance in the barn when I pretended to be sick was award-worthy. But Jennie is on an entirely other level. She's an enchantress weaving a tale and I'm just her admiring audience, standing and watching her do her magic in the middle of the library.

"So, you see, after a long talk with Rafa, he realized that I was right. That the universe's continued survival was more important than his summer vacation. That we couldn't risk all the things that have been changing to become permanent. It's as simple as using Mom's computer to book him a flight for tomorrow, and then Mr. Marcus can take him straight to the airport in Santa Fe. So Rafa's agreed to go back home. Just as long as *he* goes back to his time first," Jennie says, pointing to the man in the green sweater.

"Manolo," Marcus says.

"What?" I ask, raising my eyebrow.

"We're calling him Manolo, to avoid confusion," he explains.

Jennie waves her hands in dismissal. "It doesn't matter what we call him. Because he's going back to 2062."

Manolo still sits at the table, hunched over and gripping the fabric of his pants. He looks at me, his eyes searching. "You're really going back home? To Miami?"

I nod. "Yeah, I am. I don't like it here anyways. Too much poop, and the food isn't great."

I can't bring myself to make eye contact with Marcus or Ms. Kim.

Manolo gets up slowly from the table. He shoves his hands in his pockets and flips his hair off his forehead. "If you're leaving, then I have no reason to stay here. My job is done. I should go back before anything else gets messed up." He paused. "I just thought I might be able to see . . ."

I wait for Manolo to finish, but he bites his lip. I nod at him. "Okay, deal."

"But you'd better actually go home," Jennie says, "or Rafa will adopt fifty kittens, and then you'll end up having to care for them when they're super old and can't find the litter box."

I smirk. "What she said."

Manolo begins to walk out of the library but stops in front of me. I step back, feeling an odd sensation swirl up between us.

He looks right at me and sighs. "You understand I did this for your own good, right? For *our* own good?"

I'm not sure what he's talking about. The way I see it, he had gotten himself into some kind of time-traveling predicament and ended up causing problems here.

This whole 'you have to go home' spiel is just an excuse. One I don't get.

I don't say any of that to him, though. I just want him to leave.

Manolo raises his head to Marcus and Ms. Kim. "I'll go back tomorrow morning. I have a device that expands the wormhole I'm using to travel. It should stabilize enough to reset everything that's been changed, and we won't have done anything permanent."

He walks out of the library, and Jennie and I follow him.

I watch Manolo walk down the path, away from the library and toward the prayer labyrinth. A bright blanket of stars covers us. I look over at the elderberry shrub outside the library and spot bright pink blooms burst from its branches.

Ms. Kim told me the tree only blooms in early April and its flowers are white.

I grab Jennie's hand, hoping we made the right choice.

CHAPTER 19

YOU CAN ACCOMPLISH a lot when you're not being sabotaged by your future self. Jennie and I came up with an entirely new system to hide more snacks in the library, which makes Ms. Kim think we've suddenly become passionate about promoting books on the ranch. In reality, we've realized that the more books we place facing out on the shelves, the easier it is to hide bags of shrimp chips and chiviricos behind them. And Marcus has taught me how to apply ointment under horses' tails so that they don't get butt fungus. It's probably the most disgusting thing I've ever done.

I can't wait to email Beto and Yesi about it on Ms. Kim's computer.

But Frankie's coat is still brown. The Gearhart brothers' food is still noticeably spiceless. And Jennie's family photo still features an old white dude instead of her real dad.

Whenever I walk from my room to the library, the barn, or the dining hall, I scan for Manolo behind every building and cactus. I never see him. Jennie says that things still being out of place might just be aftereffects of us being together.

I wonder how long it'll take for our universe-ending ripples to smooth out.

Two days after my encounter with my future self, I head to the barn again, ready to slather foul-smelling cream on Frankie's hind end. As I'm grabbing the bottle of ointment out of the tack room, I hear heavy steps shuffle down the barn aisle. But before I can make a joke to Marcus about touching horses' butts, Manolo bursts into the room.

"We have a problem," he says, out of breath as he flips his hair off his forehead.

I drop the cream and it splatters on the concrete floor. "What are you still doing here? You said you would go back!"

Manolo narrows his eyes at me. "You said the same thing. And yet here we are."

I stomp, my toes stinging. "Why are you so determined to get me to go home? I don't buy the world-ending reality nonsense, even if things *are* still weird on the ranch. If it was so important for us not to be together, you wouldn't be right next to me now. So spit it out: What's the real story?"

Manolo bites his lip and counts his fingers at his side. I shake my hands to stop myself from doing the same thing. When he looks at me, his expression softens. "Please don't make me tell you. Just go back to Miami. Go back to Mom."

I open my mouth to respond, but a shout from outside the tack room stops me.

"Alvarez! Get out here!"

I shuffle out of the tack room, making sure not to brush against Manolo, and find Marcus standing at the entrance to the barn.

"In about two minutes, we're gonna be kidnapped," Marcus says when I run up to him.

"What?"

"Just be ready." He winks as I hear stomping come up the middle of the barn.

I turn and see Jennie, decked out in sunglasses, shorts, and a Grand Canyon T-shirt instead of her usual UNM hoodie. Her only correct hoodie must be dirty.

"So are you ready to go?" she asks, hands on her

hips. "This is only, like, the most fun thing we do every month."

"Are we going to get ice cream again?" I ask her. I glance back at the tack room and spot Manolo slipping from the room and out of the barn. I swallow hard and wonder if I should tell Jennie and Marcus that he's still on the ranch.

Before I can decide, Jennie slaps my arm. "No, that's on Fridays. Today's the fifteenth. It's the day we go swimming! You're not allowed to say no, either. Mr. Marcus learned a long time ago that resistance is futile."

I look from Jennie to Marcus and he shrugs.

"I don't have swim trunks. I was told, repeatedly, that this wasn't supposed to be a vacation," I tell Jennie.

She waves her hand. "Wear shorts."

"I don't have a towel."

"You're really reaching now. I have one you can use."

Marcus pats me on the back. "I know you were excited about taking care of Frankie's backside, Alvarez, but it looks like your plans for the day have been decided. Mine too."

Jennie claps. "See, Mr. Marcus? You're, like, the smartest person I know. Meet me at the creek in ten minutes!"

She turns and skips from the barn as the horses huff behind her in their stalls.

Marcus motions toward my cabin with his chin. "Better go get ready. She'll rain hellfire down on us if we're late."

I run to my room, looking up and down the path for Manolo, and change into some shorts. When I meet Marcus back at the barn, he's wearing basketball shorts and a T-shirt, but still has his dusty work boots on. The long scar on his calf snakes up his leg, and I catch myself staring at it.

Marcus clears his throat as we walk away from the barn and over a hill. "You know," he says as we round a corner around some bushes, "you shouldn't cover up the horrifying scar above your eyebrow with your hair. How else will people know you fought an actual door?"

I choke on the dry air and laugh. I look at the scar on Marcus's leg again. "I agree."

But I wonder about the scars that people can't see.

The other scars Marcus has that are hard to talk about. The ones Mom has that have nothing to do with being poked with needles all day.

I hear rushing water as we come over the top of the hill and Marcus grabs my arm. "One more thing, Alvarez. There's a reason we're going swimming today. It's because it's the fifteenth. We go swimming every month on the fifteenth."

"Why's that?"

"It's for Jennie's dad. He died on February fifteenth. She always likes to distract herself whenever this day comes around."

All thoughts of Manolo, going home, and reality-bending evaporate from my mind.

"Every single month?" I ask. "What does she do in the winter?"

"I usually take her for a trail ride. We both have people we like to remember."

Marcus and I head down toward the creek and I spot Jennie. She has three towels laid out on the edge of the creek. She's standing knee-deep in the water, letting it rush around her legs.

Waving when she sees us, Jennie shouts, "Oh my

gosh, the water is super perfect! You're gonna love it, Rafa."

I wave back at her but whisper to Marcus. "Do I say anything? Like about her dad?"

Marcus shrugs. "Sometimes I think she's trying to talk her way out of her sadness. Like if she just keeps spewing a flood of words, she'll forget the actual words she really wants to say."

"What does Jennie really want to say?"

"That she misses her dad."

Marcus and I head down to Jennie and he says, "Just enjoy the day with her. That's what she needs."

And so I do.

Jennie and I take turns splashing Marcus in the creek until he returns fire and completely drenches us. We challenge each other to jump from rock to rock across the water. Marcus makes it in two jumps, Jennie in five.

I fall in after the first rock.

Jennie cackles as I surface.

I shake my hair and spray her with water. "Yeah, I knew that wasn't gonna go well. I was so scared of falling in that—"

"You fell in?" Jennie says, winking.

I don't bother telling them I thought I'd break my ankle on a rock, or catch pneumonia, or get eaten by a rare species of New Mexico creek fish.

I shrug. "I guess I can't be like El Capitán América here and not scared of anything at all," I say, and point to Marcus.

He winds his towel and flicks it at me. "You serious, Alvarez? I'm scared of plenty."

Jennie plants her hands on her hips as she comes out of the water. "I don't believe that, Mr. Marcus. There's no way you're afraid of anything. Like, it's not humanly possible."

"Wanna bet?" Marcus holds up his hand and starts to count. "Raisins pretending to be chocolate chips, MREs past their expiration date, dudes who play soldier, and horses with bad digestion. Oh, and microwaves."

I chuckle. "Microwaves? Really?"

"I don't trust them."

Jennie laughs and kicks water at Marcus, which he dodges. "Mine is worse. And of course it's way worse than microwaves. I mean, seriously," she says. "My biggest fear is a world without snacks. Like, no thank you, sign me up to live on Mars, please."

Marcus and Jennie look at me and I bite my lip. I don't really want to share my list of things I'm afraid of. We'd be standing next to this creek until after the sun went down. "Um," I stammer, trying not to mention the fear that surprised me in the tack room. "Maybe not getting to play The Forgotten Age again? Or not getting to eat the quesitos my mom makes?"

Jennie grabs my hand as I come out of the water and squeezes it. I realize what I said, and a lump forms in my throat.

"Maybe your mom could teach you how to make them? That way you'd always know how," Jennie says. "No matter what."

I can't look her in the eye.

Marcus crams his feet back into his work boots. "Since I'm the adult here, am I supposed to tell you some quote now about courage and bravery and all that? You know, the kind of stuff English teachers make you analyze in books?"

I shake my head and wink at Marcus. "Nah, I think we're good."

"Outstanding. Because I got nothing."

Jennie laughs and pulls me away from the creek. We leave a trail of water drops as we march back to the ranch.

"Right now, I'm scared that Mom has found all the snacks we've hidden. Especially the honey butter chips. And your sugar thingies."

"Merenguitos?"

"Yeah, those. We'd better go eat some just to be safe."

"Kim, you always have the best plans," Marcus says.

As we stomp back toward the library, shaking water off our heads, I think about asking Mom about her quesito recipe when I get home. And maybe her pastelitos, too. That way I'll always have something she used to make for me.

Just in case.

Marcus hops off the path and heads toward the barn, but Jennie and I keep going, our stomachs grumbling for snacks. "Now I'm feeling like the biography section," Jennie calls over her shoulder as I follow her.

"Sweet-potato chips?"

Jennie shakes her head. "Pumpkin candies."

"That sounds good." I pick up the pace, but Jennie starts running.

"First to the library gets the most!" she shouts.

We run as fast as we can and burst through the library doors.

"Excuse me!" a woman says as we skid to a stop in front of her. She has short white hair and silver-rimmed glasses. Her mouth is pursed in a tight line. "This library isn't a playground. And it certainly isn't a place for soaking wet children."

"S-sorry," Jennie stammers. Our gaze falls to the woman's gray blouse and the Rancho Espanto name tag pinned on the fabric.

LISA KIM

"You're Lisa Kim?" I ask, blinking.

The woman gives a quick nod.

"Yes. I'm the librarian here on the ranch."

CHAPTER 20

WE MAKE IT ten feet from the library before Jennie throws up on my shoes.

I grab her arms to keep her from falling over as she mumbles, "Who is that? Where's my mom? Where's my mom?"

My hands shake as I hold on to her and I squeeze my eyes shut, trying to keep my balance. "I don't know."

Jennie wipes her mouth with the back of her hand. "It's like the photo of my dad. Except this time, Rafa, it's happening now. With someone who should exist right here."

I nod, still holding on to Jennie. "He . . . Manolo . . . is still on the ranch. He has to have something to do with this."

Jennie looks at me, her eyes darting across my face. She wrenches her arms out of my grip and pushes me aside. I stumble backward as she runs from me, but I know exactly where she's headed.

The prayer labyrinth.

I chase after Jennie, wondering how an entire person could take on a completely different appearance. A person seems a much bigger deal than a horse like Frankie. The woman in the library has to be Lisa Kim in name only. She didn't recognize Jennie as her daughter. Is she some strange alternate reality Lisa Kim who doesn't even have a kid? Is the real Ms. Kim gone forever?

It was so much simpler when I thought all of this was because of the ghost of Bartlett Arnoldson.

When Jennie and I reach the prayer labyrinth, the rocks in the maze are in a completely different design. Jennie's head jerks left and right as she scans around the labyrinth.

And then she screams.

"You!"

Running behind the twisted tree struck by lightning, Jennie throws herself at Manolo, pounding her fists into his chest. He stumbles backward onto the dirt, the metal box I saw him holding before tumbling to the ground.

"Bring her back! Make her come back!" she yells until her voice starts to scratch.

I race behind Jennie and pull on her T-shirt, trying to get her off Manolo without touching him. I don't want a repeat of the last time we made contact.

I yank Jennie off him and she doubles over, sobbing.

Manolo breathes hard, his chest heaving. He raises a shaky hand and points at me.

"It's his fault, you know," he says. "It's all his fault."

"What are you talking about?" I ask as Jennie turns and buries her head in my shoulder, her tears soaking into my sleeve.

Manolo lowers his hand and counts his fingers. "If you hadn't been obsessed with that stupid game . . . If you had cared about anything else but that . . . If you hadn't decided to do something so dumb at school . . ."

I take a deep breath. "I wouldn't have been sent here. Why does that matter so much?"

Jennie lifts her head and sniffles. "I don't care about that. I don't care what Rafa did or why he did it. All I care about is getting my mom back."

She wipes her nose with the back of her hand and clenches her fist, stepping toward Manolo, ready to strike him again.

He stands and grabs her wrists, his face red as he breathes hard.

"You're not the only one who's lost their mother!" he screams.

This time it's my turn to throw up.

My throat burns and I cough as I put my hands on my knees. Tears stream from my eyes as I gag.

He steps toward me, but I shake my head, not wanting to hear anything else he has to say.

"This was her last summer," he says, his breath hot in my ear. "This was your last chance to spend time with her, but you wasted it. Because you did something stupid. Because you'd rather be here playing with horses than see her one last time."

I squeeze my eyes shut and hear Jennie gasp. Her feet scuff in the dirt as she comes to my side. I feel her wrap her arms around me, and I dig my fingers into her shoulders and don't let go.

"Oh no, Rafa," she says.

All this time. All this time the man in the green sweater, Manolo, me. He wasn't just trying to get me kicked off the ranch. He was trying to get me to go home.

Because this is the last summer I'll get to spend with my mom.

My mom is going to die.

At this thought, I fall on the ground. I scrape my fingers in the dirt and wince as my nails sting.

No, he's wrong. Manolo has to be wrong.

I reach up and wrap my hand around his forearm. His eyes widen as heat bursts under my fingers.

A rhythmic beep fills my ears. I see flowers. Long, blurry black figures. One of the figures approaches and a face focuses. It's Dad. He opens his mouth to speak, but his chin quivers and he shakes his head.

I gasp and let go of Manolo's arm. We're both sprawled on the ground, breathing hard.

Manolo looks at me, tears in his eyes. "You see it, don't you?" he asks.

"What was that?" My fingers still sting and my stomach rumbles. I swallow hard, afraid I might throw up again.

"My memories. It's what I remember from Mom's funeral."

Jennie brings her arms around me again and squeezes. I don't want her to let go.

The three of us sit crouched on the ground as the sun starts to set behind the canyon walls. A lizard runs across the labyrinth, oblivious to the path outlined by the rocks and perches on a stone, staring at us. His body shivers and he raises his head as he bursts into dozens of butterflies that flit around us. The sight would be pretty if it wasn't so horrifying.

I squeeze my eyes shut, not wanting to witness any more of our reality warping. Cricket chirps fill the air and I try to focus on their sound, but the rhythm reminds me of the beeps in Manolo's memory and my heart thuds in my chest.

"How do I fix this? How do I change my future?" I whisper.

Manolo grimaces and shakes his head. "You can't. It's already happened."

I feel Jennie's grip tighten around me. I want to bury my head in her shoulder and sob. I think of the silliest thing—Mom's quesitos. I was so excited about asking her teach me how to make them.

So I'm not going to get to eat them again? I'm not going to help Mom out in her sculpture studio any-more? No more snorkeling trips to Key Largo so she

243

can sketch coral reefs. No more asking me about my latest adventure in The Forgotten Age.

She'll just be . . . gone.

I squeeze my eyes shut and concentrate on my breathing, trying not to throw up again.

New Mexico has never felt farther away from Miami than it does right now. I can't do anything for Mom all the way out here. I can't make things better. I can't change what Manolo tells me is going to happen, and has already happened for him.

I stand up, pulling Jennie with me.

I can't do anything for my own mom all the way out here in New Mexico, but I can still help Jennie's.

Brushing the dirt off my pants, I look at Manolo. "We have to figure out how to get Jennie's mom back. It's both of our faults that Ms. Kim is gone."

Manolo stands and looks at Jennie. His eyes soften and for the first time, I recognize the face I see when I look in the mirror.

"I have to go back to my time. If my theories are correct, everything should go back to how it was once I leave. Kind of like a reset button. But I have to go soon, or I'm afraid the changes will be irreversible."

Jennie finally speaks up. "So leave. Now. I want my mom back."

Manolo sighs, bending over to pick something off the ground.

"There's a slight problem with that. I couldn't leave before because the device I use to pinpoint and stabilize wormholes needed negative energy to charge. But there hasn't been a storm here since the day I arrived. I was trying to find another source for the past two days, but nothing will work. I tried to tell Rafa that this morning."

"What's negative energy?" I ask.

Manolo takes a deep breath. "It's not exactly what it sounds like. It's not negatively charged energy, it's simply a different form of it. Scientists from your time have been theorizing about it for decades, but in mine, we've actually discovered how to utilize it."

As I try to understand what Manolo is saying, I resist reminding him that I almost failed science last year. "So you need this negative energy for your device?"

Manolo nods. "Yes. There are large pools of negative energy above powerful thunderstorms, and my device is able to draw that energy and charge during a storm. But now there's another problem . . ."

Manolo holds out his hand and shows us the metal box he first told us about in the library. It's still the same shoebox-sized machine, but it has a large scuff one side.

"When I fell to the ground just now," Manolo says, looking at Jennie, "my device broke."

Manolo opens up the back of the box, and Jennie and I step closer to look inside. A thick metal coil rattles around the parts of the box as Manolo moves his hand.

"That coil needs to be put back in place, but I have no idea how to do it here, in the middle of the ranch, even if we had the right tools. My partner in the lab where I work helped me make this device. I'm more of a big-idea person, not so much a nuts-and-bolts person."

I hold out my hand to Manolo. "Can I see it?"

He gives the box to me, careful to make sure our fingers don't touch. I inspect the parts. There are small mirrors and what looks like pieces from the inside of a computer. The metal coil has snapped off from two metal brackets.

I know how to fix this.

And Manolo should, too.

"The coil just needs to be soldered back to the brackets. Assuming we can find a torch here on the ranch somewhere, it should be a quick fix."

Manolo looks at me. "You know how to solder?"

I scrunch my eyebrows together. "Of course I do. Solder, weld, braze. All of it. You should, too. Mom taught us."

"Mom . . . taught us?" he asks slowly.

"Yeah," I say, annoyed. "Because she's a *metal sculpture artist.*"

Manolo's mouth drops open and he shakes his head.

"No, she's not," he says, his eyes darting from the device to me. "She's a graphic novelist."

CHAPTER 21

WHAT THE ACTUAL babosan bomb?

My head hurts.

Manolo, Jennie, and I walk back to the barn in silence.

A bright yellow-blue-and-red bird flies across our path, so close that its wings rustle my hair. It reminds me of the birds that always get loose from Jungle Island in Miami. As my eyes follow the bird, I realize it actually is a parrot.

And it shouldn't be in northeastern New Mexico.

The bird perches in a sprawling palm tree, another plant that seems to be growing far from its original habitat.

The number of things changing because of Manolo and me seems to be increasing. And there's no way we can hide all of this from everyone on the ranch.

For some reason, all I can think about are the

alosynths from The Forgotten Age, creatures that can morph and change their appearance. Just like what happened with Frankie and Ms. Kim. And maybe Mom, too?

I want to ask Manolo so many things. What happens to Mom? How much time do I have with her? What happens . . . after?

But the pounding in my head keeps my words from coming together. They jumble up in my brain, mixed with the memory I saw when I grabbed Manolo's arm.

But if he said Mom is a graphic novelist, when the Mirta Alvarez I know is an artist, then are we even talking about the same person?

Is it like the white-haired, sour-looking Lisa Kim being another version of the Lisa Kim that's Jennie's mom?

So many thoughts and so many questions. But if I could open my mouth, only one sentence would come out.

I want my mom.

I look at Manolo as he counts his fingers and chews on the side of his mouth. He hasn't said anything since we left the labyrinth, but I can tell he's deep in thought as his eyebrows knit together.

Jennie is still holding my hand as she tugs on the hem of her T-shirt with her other hand. She breathes hard and blows her purple bangs off her forehead.

When we pass the library, I notice her peer in the window, looking to see if the woman who is supposed to be Lisa Kim is still in there.

Jennie and I lead Manolo to the barn, to try to find Marcus, to put the wormhole device back together, to try to fix everything that's been made wrong.

Our steps are heavy under the weight of what we have to do.

Mom would tell me the easiest way to eat an entire pan of pastelitos de guayaba is to do it one bite at a time.

So making sure I don't pass out on our way to the barn is the first bite.

I take deep breaths as we look for Marcus. Walking down the barn aisle, I inspect each stall, wondering if any other horses have changed color.

Turns out coat color is the least of my worries. Ike is gone from his stall and replaced by a donkey,

Wattson's stall has two llamas, and there's a zebra in Jiji's stall. An actual zebra.

I have to fix this before anyone sees that our barn has turned into a zoo.

We can't find Marcus anywhere. My stomach sinks, and I hope he hasn't changed, too.

"It's late," Jennie finally says. Her voice is soft and shaky, so unlike the usual storm of words filled with energy. I hardly recognize it. "He probably went to his trailer."

And so we walk again and I take another bite, willing my legs not to give out as they shake from nervousness.

Marcus's trailer sits nestled between scraggly bushes. When we approach the wooden steps outside his door, I watch a long snake slither out from underneath and I jump back. I almost grab Manolo's arm, but he steps away from me as he eyes the snake warily.

But then the snake's body shakes. Its scaled skin writhes as black spots burst from its body. I watch in horror as the snake explodes into hundreds of spiders, crawling everywhere across the dirt and rocks.

Another twist of reality caused by Manolo and me being near each other.

"Nope. That's it. I'm done," I say as I march up the steps to Marcus's trailer and bang on the door.

When Marcus answers he looks from Jennie to me. His eyes fall on Manolo and he frowns.

"You good, Alvarez?" he asks. And then he looks above my head and into the sky. His eyes grow wide and his mouth drops open. "What the . . . ?"

I turn to see what he's looking at and gasp. Jennie rushes to my side again and grabs my arm as Manolo doubles over, his hands resting on his knees as he shakes his head.

"It's too much. We're too close. We have to fix this," he mumbles.

Hanging high in the black night sky above our heads are two full moons. Not one like there should be. Two.

"Yeah, so obviously everything is upside down and horrible," I say as I turn back to Marcus, shaking my head to fling the image of lunar nightmare from my brain. "We need your help."

Marcus comes out of his trailer and down the steps. He squashes a stray spider under his boot, barely taking his eyes off the sky.

"What's going on?"

I don't think he's seen what's in the barn yet, and I can only hope that everyone else on the ranch stays sound asleep in their rooms so they don't see the double moon.

Manolo steps forward and clears his throat. He tells Marcus all about needing negative energy to charge his device that locates and stabilizes wormholes. He shows Marcus the coil that broke loose from the inside of the machine when he fell.

"Rafa says he can fix it if we can find a welder here on the ranch. Because he knows how to do that sort of thing," Manolo says.

Marcus raises an eyebrow. "Wouldn't you know how to do it, too? Since you're the same person," he says, letting out a long breath. "I can't believe saying stuff like that is normal now. But then again . . ."

He gestures broadly at the night sky and sighs.

I scuff my shoes in the dirt. "Yeah, about that. Turns out we have different moms."

Jennie squeezes my hand at the word *mom* but stays silent.

Marcus shakes his head. "What are you talking about?"

Clearing his throat, Manolo finally stops counting his fingers. "I've been thinking about it and I'm pretty sure Rafa and I are proof of the existence of multiverses. Even though we're the same person, our realities are different. It's like a tree. For each decision that's made, a new branch forms. Choose one decision, you go one way on the branch. Choose a different option, another branch is formed. There are endless branches because we're faced with hundreds of decisions each day. And even the smallest choice can change things."

Manolo looks at me and a sympathetic smile breaks out on his face. "The mom that I know, the Mirta Alvarez from my time, is not necessarily the same Mirta Alvarez from this time."

"My mom is a metal sculpture artist. That's how I know how to weld," I explain. "But his mom is a graphic novelist."

Marcus lets out another long breath and puts his hands on his hips, taking it all in. He looks at Jennie and raises an eyebrow. "Kim, how are you not bouncing all over the place right now? This is exactly the sort of thing you love."

Jennie lets go of my hand. She opens her mouth to speak, but her chin starts to quiver and her shoulders shake. She rushes to Marcus and sobs into his chest as he wraps his arms around her.

"What happened, Alvarez?" Marcus asks. He pats Jennie's purple hair, which has come completely loose from her braids.

"Ms. Kim is gone," I whisper. "There's some old white lady in the library whose name tag says LISA KIM. All these changes on the ranch because Manolo and I are here at the same time, and now it seems like a Lisa Kim from another multiverse or whatever has replaced Jennie's mom."

"What?"

Jennie sniffs and holds on tighter to Marcus. "She's not there. My mom's gone, and now I don't have anybody."

Marcus swallows hard as he holds on to Jennie. I can't read his face as he stares straight ahead. I glance at Manolo, but his eyes are fixed on the ground, kicking away a spider that scurried across the path.

I look back at Marcus, his short cut hair, his linebacker shoulders, his permanently dusty jeans. I don't want him to disappear. I don't want him to go away. He's all we have right now.

Finally, Marcus pulls Jennie from him. "Let's go, Kim. It's gonna be okay."

Marcus's long legs stride him so purposefully away from the trailer that we have to hurry to keep up with him. I look over at Manolo and realize he's struggling to keep up.

Apparently, my stamina doesn't improve as I get older.

Marcus leads us to a shed behind the barn and throws open the doors. We stand outside as we hear him rummaging inside, metal clanking as he grumbles.

"Here it is," he says, emerging from the shed with a small acetylene torch, welder's helmet, and a pair of gloves. "The guy I replaced used to fix the fencing with this. Left it here and told me I shouldn't use it if I didn't know how or I'd blow myself up. Made it ten years in the military without doing that so I wasn't about to try now in the middle of New Mexico."

I take the torch from Marcus and examine it. This is just like the one Mom first taught me how to use.

There are two tanks, each with a rubber hose that both connect to what looks like a flashlight with a bent metal straw on the end.

"You sure you know how to use this?" Marcus asks. "*Without* causing an explosion?"

I nod, examining the hoses for any cracks or holes. "Yeah. This'll be easy. I used to help Mom in her studio. Especially after she started to get sick."

Manolo examines my face. I feel like he's searching for a memory he can't find.

"You never did that, did you?" I ask him, turning the valves on each tank to start the flow of gas.

He shakes his head. "After she got sick, I was in charge of organizing the sketches she did for her books."

I chew on my lip and think, examining the gauges on the acetylene and oxygen cylinders to make sure the gas is flowing. "Then why do we have the same memories of what we said to her after she got the news from the doctors? How do we know the same things about The Forgotten Age?"

"Maybe some of our branches overlap," Manolo says, shrugging.

Marcus groans. "I'm just gonna pretend I know what you're talking about. So what do you need to do to fix that thing?"

I peek into the shed and see a metal table. "I should probably work on that. I don't really want to solder in the barn with all the dry hay in there."

"Not setting the barn on fire is a good goal," Marcus says.

Manolo places the device on the table. I slip the leather glove over my hand and place the welding helmet on my head. The chirps of crickets, the snorts of animals in the barn, and Jennie's nervous foot tapping in the dirt fade away. I find a striker on a shelf above the table and squeeze it in front of the tip of the torch. Sparks fly and a long flame shoots from the end. I always used to jump when that happened, but it quickly became my favorite part of the process.

Focusing on Manolo's machine, I inspect the loose coil. I know how to fix this. One time I got mad when Dad told me I spent too much time at Beto's house playing The Forgotten Age. I stomped into Mom's shop to complain and knocked over a piece she'd been working on—tall, delicate reeds that looked like they were swaying in the wind. The top of one reed snapped off when it crashed to the concrete floor. Instead of getting angry, Mom showed me how to fix it.

As I heat up the end of the bracket and coil until they glow, I remember how she had stood behind me, her hand on my shoulder.

"Now touch the solder to the ends you've heated up, Pollito," I hear Mom say.

I take a roll of solder from the shelf in front of me and connect it to the bracket and the coil. It heats up and liquefies when it comes in contact with the glowing pieces. The melted solder builds up between the coil and the bracket and connects them.

"It's simple, Pollito," I hear Mom chuckle. "Anything broken can be fixed. It may not look exactly like it did before, but it'll be its own version of whole."

Just as I turn the torch off and remove my helmet and glove, I hear Marcus shout from outside the shed, "Hey, Alvarez. You need to hurry up. Something's happening."

I watch as the shed walls start to quiver and shake, nails flying through the air. I grab the device and jump through the doorway just as the shed vanishes with a loud pop.

Jennie shakes her head. "No. Nothing else can disappear. Nothing."

I catch my breath and show the inside of the device to Manolo. "I think it's fixed, right?"

Manolo nods and closes the device, twisting the screws in the corners. "Now it just needs to charge and I can go back."

"And reset everything to the way it was," Jennie says behind us.

Marcus walks over to her. "You can stay with me, Kim. Until your mom comes back. Which she will."

I look at Manolo. "So now what?"

He holds the device close to his chest. "We need to figure out when the next storm will be. Hopefully, it'll be soon."

"We can look up the weather forecast on the computer in my mom's office in the library," Jennie says. "Assuming that the lady in there will let us."

Marcus grabs Jennie's hand. "Shouldn't be a problem, Kim. It's after dark. The library's closed and locked up. You know how many times I had to pick locks on shipping containers so we wouldn't have to wait for some clipboard-obsessed Chairborne Ranger? We're good."

So once again our traveling quartet marches across the ranch, past a normally rushing creek now dusty and dry and palm trees that belong hundreds of miles from here. I spot a black shadow darting from behind the library and around the elderberry shrub still covered in pink flowers. I can't make out exactly what it is, and with everything changing on the ranch, I'm not sure I want to find out.

I can only hope our traveling band of warrior, healer, mage, and rogue can fix everything.

CHAPTER 22

MARCUS WAS RIGHT. He *is* an expert at picking locks. Not that the Rancho Espanto library had a lock that could withstand a Forgotten Age warrior anyways.

I start to turn the light on, but Jennie grabs my hand. "No. People will realize we're in here. I don't want that woman to come."

Squinting at the lack of light in the library, I notice that entire bookshelves have disappeared. Whole sections of poetry, graphic novels, and mysteries have vanished. As my eyes adjust, I see they've been replaced by large posters advertising a reality dating show competition.

Ms. Kim, the real Ms. Kim, would absolutely hate this.

We head to Ms. Kim's office and turn the computer on, the four of us crammed in the small space. I make a point of not making contact with Manolo and he edges to the other side of Marcus.

Jennie sits at the computer and pulls up the weather forecast in a browser.

"I don't know what we're gonna do if there's a drought," Jennie says. "So cross your fingers, everybody."

"And your toes," Marcus adds.

"And your butt cheeks," I say.

Manolo rolls his eyes and I can't help but shake my head. "Yeah, I know. It sucks being us," I tell him.

Jennie drags her finger across the screen, scanning the forecast. She gasps. "Someone else look at this and tell me my eyes aren't playing tricks on me."

I lean over her shoulder. "Nope. You're right. This says there's going to be a storm."

"When?" Manolo asks.

I look at him and grin. "Tomorrow morning."

Jennie puts her head in her hands and sighs. Marcus squeezes her shoulder.

"C'mon, Kim. I've got cup ramen we can gorge ourselves on while we wait. It's your fault I'm addicted to it anyways," he says. Then he bites his lip and adds,

"Assuming it's still cup ramen in my pantry and not twelve different flavors of creamed soup."

A smile breaks out on Jennie's face for the first time in hours. "We'd better go check. Two bags of Hi-Chew say I can eat more ramen than you."

Marcus laughs and pats her on the back. "You're on."

They shuffle out of Ms. Kim's office, and Manolo starts to follow them.

"Manolo," I say, even though it still feels weird to call him that. "Hang on."

I sit down at the computer and pull up the video chat site I use with Mom. I send her a quick request even though I know it's late in Miami.

"What are you doing?" Manolo asks.

"This is why you came here, right?" I drag a chair next to me at the computer and motion for him to sit down. When he does, the computer buzzes and I see Mom has accepted my request. Her face pops up on the screen and Manolo gasps.

"Ay, mi Pollito. ¿Cómo anda? It's so late," Mom says. Her cheeks are sunken and she's not wearing one of her scarves, her bald head reflecting the light from her computer screen.

Manolo covers his mouth as he leans away from the computer camera so Mom won't see him.

"Yeah, I know it's late. Sorry about that," I tell Mom. "I just thought maybe this was one of your no-sleep nights. And I wanted to chat."

Mom smiles and nods. "Ño ñoña, you thought right. Not much sleep going on here. The doctor put me on a new medication que me dio una bofetada."

I chuckle. "Sorry it's kicking your butt. That sucks."

Manolo takes deep breaths next to me as he calms down. He stares at the screen, taking in every inch of Mom's face. I catch him starting to reach his hand out to the screen, but he squeezes his fingers in a fist instead.

"So what's new with you?" Mom asks. "Is it still all horse poop, all the time?"

I chuckle. "Kind of. But it's not too bad."

Looking at Manolo, I motion for him to scoot closer to me. "Actually, I wanted to introduce you to someone."

Manolo stares at me with wide eyes glistening with tears. "I don't think I can do this," he whispers.

I point to him even though Mom still can't see him.

"This is Dr. Manolo. He's this really cool scientist I met here on the ranch."

Manolo quickly wipes his eyes and moves his chair in front of the computer camera. He gives Mom a shy wave. "Hi, Ms. Alvarez. Nice to meet you," he says, his voice shaky.

Mom brushes her hand across her head, realizing she's not covered up. "Oh, hi," she says. "Nice to meet you, too. Sorry about my appearance. I've had better days."

Manolo smiles. He looks younger than his fifty-two years. "It's okay."

"Dr. Manolo is doing some research on the ranch and I got to help him a little," I tell Mom.

She laughs and Manolo takes a deep breath in at the sound. "That's good," she says. "We should email your science teacher and tell her. Maybe get you some extra credit. He didn't do the best last year. I bet a scientist like you always got good grades."

"Actually, I used to do terribly in science," Manolo says. Like me, he was distracted by long hospital stays, chores at home, and bad news. "But I got better. It was my mom who inspired me to be a scientist. I wanted to learn how to fix things. How to make things better."

Mom smiles and nods. "I'm sure she's proud of you."

Manolo sighs and his chin quivers again. He's gripping the fabric on his pants with white knuckles. I want to grab his hand and squeeze it to let him know he'll be okay. That we'll be okay.

"I hope she is," he finally manages.

Mom waves her hand. "Of course she is. That's how moms are. This one here," she says, pointing to me, "drives me completamente loca sometimes, but I'd still make quesitos for him anytime he asks."

I smile at her. "I got to weld today to help out Dr. Manolo. A piece of his equipment was broken and I fixed it by soldering the pieces back together."

Mom claps and giggles. The sound makes my stomach jump. "Así es! That's wonderful!"

Manolo rubs his chin. "He saved my whole research project. I can see him becoming an artist just like you one day. Or maybe a scientist like me. Or anything at all, really."

I look at Manolo and it hits me. His path isn't necessarily mine. If we're from different timelines, then

I don't have to become a scientist. I can be whatever I want. I'm not locked into some preset path.

And if I'm not stuck with an already determined future, maybe Mom isn't, either.

A glimmer of hope starts to grow low in my belly, and I inhale until I think my lungs might burst.

Mom yawns and slowly shakes her head. "I think I'd better head to bed now. But I'm so glad we got to chat. It made my night."

"It was nice to meet you, Ms. Alvarez," Manolo says. He's leaning toward the computer, as if he wants to dive right through the screen and give Mom a hug. I don't blame him. I want to do the same thing.

Mom studies Manolo's face, her forehead wrinkling in concentration. "You know, Manolo is my son's middle name."

Manolo looks down sheepishly. "Yeah, we figured that out."

Mom's eyes dart from me to Manolo, taking in the scars over our eyebrows, the way our mouths pull down on one side when we smile, how we flip our hair off our forehead.

The smallest gasp escapes her throat.

I worry that it might be too much for her. I worry that we've overwhelmed her.

But a smile tugs at the corner of her mouth.

"You know, Dr. Manolo, I'm glad Rafa got to work with you on the ranch. That he got to meet someone so intelligent and accomplished. Someone trying to answer big questions and solve problems. I've always admired people like that."

Manolo sucks in a breath and blinks repeatedly as tears pool in his eyes.

Mom looks at him through the screen with a sympathetic smile. "Your mom is most definitely proud of you. I know I would be."

She turns her gaze to me. "And I'm proud of you, too, Pollito. When you come home, we'll work on a piece together. I'll start sketching it out."

I nod. "Only if you can. It's okay if you're too tired. We'll have time."

I stop myself and swallow hard. I hope we do have time.

Manolo and I say goodbye to Mom, staring at the computer screen together long after we're disconnected.

"Thank you," Manolo whispers, his head in his hands. "Thank you for that."

I want to pat his back, but I know better. "I wanted to see her. So I figured you did, too."

Tears seep through Manolo's fingers. "It's been so long. I'd forgotten what she looked like. I'd forgotten her smile. I couldn't picture her eyes. It's been forty years. I've been drowning myself in work, hoping maybe I could see her just one more time."

I take a deep breath.

Manolo continues. "When I realized I'd created a device that could time-travel, the first thing I wanted was to do was see Mom. I didn't know yet that whatever time I traveled to, I was going to show up wherever you were. Because we're connected. So when I ended up on this ranch, so far away from her, I was angry. I took it out on you because I remember getting sent out here myself. And I was still so mad about it. I've had this bitterness in my gut at missing out on time I could have spent with her because I just wanted to remember her so badly."

I give Manolo a small smile.

"But there's one thing I've never forgotten. One

thing that inspired me to do the work that I do. One thing I always have with me," he says.

"What's that?"

"Her stories."

Manolo and I sit in Ms. Kim's office as he tells me the stories from his mom's graphic novels. Tales of monsters chasing lost travelers, of fantastical worlds filled with magic. Of heroes who mess up and villains who aren't as bad as they seem.

All through the night, he paints his mom's books.

It's not until he finishes telling me about her last book, early in the morning, that we hear the deep rumble of thunder outside.

CHAPTER 23

MANOLO AND I run out of the library but skid to a stop in front of a man blocking the path. He turns slowly and faces us, a worn olive shirt hanging loose on his bony shoulders. He smirks, his eyes dark, and black stubble covers his jaw.

"You wanna tell me why so many pus-filled varmints are on my land?"

I stumble back and almost grab Manolo's arm. "B-Bartlett?"

The man nods slowly, his smirk growing to reveal sharp teeth. Even with the dim morning light peeking through the storm clouds, I can see the outline of the dining hall through the washed-out skin of his body.

I'm looking at a ghost.

"Run," I hear Manolo whisper behind me.

I don't need to be told twice. We take off down the path and put dust clouds between us and the actual ghost of Bartlett Arnoldson. I hear a shout behind us.

"Ain't heard from that brother of mine, have you?" Bartlett snarls.

My stomach flips-flops at the thought of what else Manolo and me being in the same reality might cook up.

I look up as thick black clouds sail overhead. At least they'll cover the two moons hanging in the sky above them. The same dark shadow I saw earlier darts from behind the dining hall and races up the path ahead of us. I still can't make out what it is, especially since the increasing storm has covered most of the morning light.

I'm not sure I want to find out. The ghost of Bartlett Arnoldson was more than enough.

"We should hurry," Manolo says, picking up the pace. "Sometimes storms can blow through kind of quickly. We can't miss this chance."

I run alongside him, my adrenaline making me forget that I've been awake since yesterday. The last time I stayed up all night was when Beto, Yesi, and I decided to watch a Zombie Alligator Squad marathon on a Tuesday. Dad still made me go to school the next day and I got in trouble for snoring in history class.

"Rafa, one more thing," Manolo says as we pass the

dining hall. A clap of thunder rumbles over the cliffs and I jump. "I've tried not to tell you too much. I don't want to influence you unnaturally. But there is one thing I need you to know."

I wonder what Manolo is about to tell me.

Do I end up tripping in the middle of a school pep rally, my pants falling as I tumble down the bleachers and expose my bare butt to the entire eighth grade?

"Don't stop playing The Forgotten Age."

"What? Really? That's what you need me to do?"

Manolo nods and reaches into his pocket. He takes out a purple twenty-sided die and rolls it between his fingers. I smile and reach into my own pocket, show-ing Manolo the exact same die.

As we walk, Manolo says, "Dad doesn't exactly handle things well after Mom . . . you know."

"You can say it. I can take it."

"After Mom died, Dad just focused on work. Being at home pretty much sucked. But whenever Beto and Yesi came over to play The Forgotten Age, I was happy. Beto even figured out Mom's quesito recipe. Just so you know, the secret is lemon juice."

"Do you still play it?" I want to ask him what Beto

and Yesi are like forty years from now, but I think that's something I'd rather find out for myself.

Manolo nods. "Yeah, there's a group of us from work that play. It's considered a vintage game now. But The Forgotten Age is actually how we came up with the idea of the wormhole device."

I think for a moment. "The divining rods in the Hedor Swamps. That's where you got it from, isn't it?"

Manolo smiles. "Exactly. I wanted to call Dad right up and tell him that all those hours we spent playing weren't a waste of time. That Mom was right all along. Our game was special."

When we reach the prayer labyrinth, the wind picks up again and I have to lift my arm to shield my eyes from the blowing dirt. The temperature has dropped ten degrees since we left the library. I shiver. A rumble fills the air and large rocks drop from the cliff face in front of us, tumbling down the side and crashing to the ground in a cloud of dust.

Manolo clears his throat and sets his wormhole device in the center of the prayer labyrinth.

I'm not sure what to expect. A bright light. Lasers shooting out of the center.

But it just lays in the dirt and buzzes.

"Is it working?" I ask.

Manolo nods. "Science isn't always fireworks. Sometimes it's . . . well, boring."

I bite my lip. "Fireworks would've been kinda cool, though."

Shaking his head, Manolo faces me. A light on the side of the device starts to blink. "It should be charged now. I . . . I think I'm ready to go."

Glancing at his hand, I see he's counting his fingers. He smiles when he notices me doing the same thing.

The humming from the device gets louder, but Manolo still stands in front of me. "I don't know what to say," he whispers sheepishly.

I shrug. "Me neither."

Manolo runs his hand through his hair. "Thank you for letting me see Mom. I'm sorry I messed up every-thing for you here on the ranch. I just missed her so much. I wanted more time with her, you know?"

"I get it. Maybe not the trying to get me stampeded by horses or buried under rocks part, but I under-stand."

Manolo casts a glance over to the wormhole device

as it starts to beep on the ground. He scuffs his shoe in the dirt. "So, I guess to make up for it, is there anything you want to ask me? Anything you want to know about the future?"

An avalanche of thoughts tumbles out of my brain and into my throat.

Will Beto, Yesi, and I ever conquer The Forgotten Age? When do I start growing an actual mustache and not just baby hairs? Will I ever not feel like I'm going to throw up when I have to talk in front of people? Will Dad ever quit rolling his eyes when I talk about my player characters?

When does Mom . . . ?

But I never say the words. Those are questions for my time, my world.

I shake my head. "I don't think you and I are really from the same world. Some things might be the same for us, but I don't think everything is."

Manolo looks me in the eye. He moves to put his hand on my shoulder but pulls his arm back.

"I hope everything isn't the same. I really do."

I start to say something, but a sharp snort fills the air. I turn and look behind me and see the dark shadow emerge from behind the lightning-struck tree. It stalks toward Manolo and me, its head darting from side to side as it sizes us up.

At first, I think it's one of the earth babies Jennie talked about, the Arnoldson brothers' stories come to life. But that's not it.

It's a dinosaur. An actual, living dinosaur.

I blink as my stomach flip-flops.

The Coelophysis is almost as tall as I am, and *way* longer. It lifts its head in the air and snorts again.

I start to wish that I had asked Jonas if Coelophysis were carnivorous until I see rows of sharp teeth bared in my direction.

"I need to get out of here before that thing snacks on our eyeballs," Manolo says.

I'd laugh at him sounding exactly like me if I wasn't busy backing away from the Triassic terror we managed to bring into our timeline.

Manolo runs to the center of the prayer labyrinth. Picking up the wormhole device, he flips a switch and the humming increases. My gaze darts from watching the Coelophysis barrel straight at me with its razor teeth to Manolo's feet slowly disappearing, followed by his legs and torso. The last thing I see is his smile as he takes the twenty-sided die from his pocket and flips it in his hand, a purple orb floating in the air as he fades.

I squeeze my eyes shut as I hear the Coelophysis launch itself into the air, ready to pounce on me. I gather my knees to my chest and scream, waiting to feel my muscles ripping from my bones.

A sharp clap of thunder breaks out overhead and I wince. I open my eyes and stare at the empty prayer labyrinth, smoke rising from the blackened tree as if it was just struck by lightning.

No dinosaur.

No Manolo.

He's gone. The man who made my life miserable for the last three weeks. The man who turned out to be me from the future. The man who lost his mom and just wanted to see her one last time.

Before I can think too much about how this has officially been the weirdest summer in the history of weird summers, a fat raindrop pelts me directly on the tip of my nose. The wind picks up and the rain falls sideways, straight into my face.

I take off running down the dirt path that's quickly turning into mud. The closest building to the prayer labyrinth is the dining hall. I sprint there as quickly as I can to get out of the storm. When I reach the porch that hangs out in front of the broad wooden building, completely out of breath, I put my hands on my knees as my shoulders heave.

And then a thought comes to me. Pushing through the door of the dining hall, I sprint back toward the kitchen where the Gearhart brothers are preparing breakfast.

Buzz-Cut Gearhart stands over a large dish of scrambled eggs and I spot bits of green chili poking out from the runny yolks. Grabbing a spoon, I dig into the mound of eggs and shove a massive bite into my mouth.

"Hey, man. Breakfast isn't ready yet," Buzz-Cut Gearhart says to me.

My tongue burns as I chew and my eyes begin to water. As I swallow, heat pricks my throat and I cough, bits of egg flying onto the tile floor of the kitchen.

They're the best-tasting eggs I've ever had in my life.

I start to laugh, and the Gearhart brothers eye me warily.

"You okay there, kid?" Long-Haired Gearhart asks.

I nod. "Best breakfast ever. Five stars. Amazing. You guys are the best cooks in all of New Mexico."

Before they can respond, I run back out of the dining hall and into the rain, my mouth still burning.

I have something else to check.

In the library.

CHAPTER 24

"**DID YOU KNOW** that the state insect of New Mexico is the tarantula hawk wasp? It's a wasp that can sting and paralyze tarantulas. Then they drag them into their nests and lay eggs on the tarantulas so that the babies can eat them while they're still alive. Like a spider buffet for wasp larvae. So awesome."

Jennie looks at me as I toss my suitcase in the bed of Marcus's truck.

"Ño, it's seven in the morning. Why do I need to know this right now?" I ask her.

She flicks a purple braid over her shoulder. "Well, you're leaving, and I realized there's so much I still haven't told you. About New Mexico. About the best books in the library, the awesomest Korean snacks, and why you're still wrong about tteokbokki not being as good as ropa vieja. I looked up what that meant. It's 'old clothes' in Spanish. Seriously, you have to be kidding me."

Before I can respond or start an argument that I know I will eventually lose to Jennie's expert verbal ability, Ms. Kim comes up to the truck and puts her arm around my shoulder.

"I brought you something for your flight home. Shockingly, I discovered it behind the photography books," she says, raising her eyebrow at Jennie.

I take a bag of coffee candies from Ms. Kim. "Thanks," I tell her. "I think I might save these for my mom, if that's okay with you. She's super obsessed with coffee. 'Como buena cubana,' she says."

Ms. Kim laughs. "Like a good Cuban. I think your mom and I would get along."

I slip the bag of candies into my backpack. Hopefully, Ms. Kim didn't find the surprise I left for Jennie: plantain chips behind the picture books, merenguitos behind the poetry section, and ajonjoli candies behind the dictionaries.

I spent the last week sneaking them into the library without Ms. Kim or Jennie finding out. After Manolo left, I had a lot more time on my hands since I wasn't trying to keep the universe from imploding anymore. Jennie clung to her Mom's side for three straight days after Ms. Kim replaced the sour-faced, white-haired lady. She didn't seem to realize she'd been gone at all.

Everything else had reset, too. The zoo of animals disappeared from the barn when Frankie's coat went back to the right color, the books in the library returned to their correct languages, Jennie's hoodies all said University of New Mexico again, and the artists' paintings stopped changing along with the rocks in the prayer labyrinth. There were no more dinosaur sightings, either.

It still gives me a headache to think about all that's happened.

"You good to go, Alvarez?" Marcus asks as he walks up to us, flipping his truck keys in his hand.

I nod. Ms. Kim steps up and pulls me into a hug. I wrap my arms around her and let her hold me. She's as short as Mom is now, and I can practically rest my head on top of hers. When I pull away, Ms. Kim puts her hands on my shoulders.

"I'm glad you got to spend some time with us this summer. Maybe we'll see you next year? Hopefully there won't be any time-travel, reality-ending nonsense and we can just focus on books and horses."

I smile. "Books and horses. I'd like that."

Jennie climbs into the cab of Marcus's truck and slides to the middle.

"You're coming, too?" I ask her.

Nodding, she says, "Of course. Mr. Marcus has to have someone to tell him where to go. He'd be lost without me."

Marcus laughs as he climbs into the driver's seat. "You're my navigator, Kim. And maybe we'll navigate ourselves to the ice cream shop in Florita after we drop Alvarez at the airport."

Jennie's eyes grow wide and she claps. "Yeah, but you're not allowed to order vanilla. Like, it's banned. Pretend it doesn't even exist. We are now living in a timeline where vanilla ice cream has been wiped from the face of the earth."

"You'll have to keep me updated on all the flavors you try," I tell Jennie.

As Marcus pulls away from the ranch and I wave to Ms. Kim, Jennie nods enthusiastically. "Of course. I can update you when we play The Forgotten Age. Brilliant idea letting me play virtually. I hope Mom is ready for me to take over her computer. And I hope your friends are ready to meet the best player character ever."

I smile as I watch the trees fly past us as Marcus drives toward Santa Fe. I can't wait for Beto and Yesi to meet Jennie, even if it'll just be through a computer screen. I'm pretty certain Jennie's energy will come shooting out anyways. And Beto and I will most likely have to hang on as Jennie and Yesi take over our adventures.

I have to prepare my player character to battle a lot more blargmores.

When Marcus drives through Florita and continues on toward Santa Fe, he clears his throat, his eyes still fixed on the road.

"You know, Alvarez, you better not forget everything I taught you about taking care of horses. Practice on an alligator or something. You got plenty of those down where you live, I'm sure."

Jennie slaps Marcus on the arm as I laugh.

I take a deep breath and watch the water rush through the creek alongside the road. Jennie wraps her hand around mine and squeezes. She rests her head on my shoulder and whispers, "Do you think maybe . . . do you think in one of those multiverses Manolo was talking about, some version of my dad is still alive?"

I squeeze Jennie's hand back. "I think so. It seems like with all the different realities there are, it's possible."

Jennie lifts her head and looks at me, smiling. "I like the idea of that."

Marcus grips the steering wheel tightly and I wonder if he's thinking about his friend, Olstead. Maybe there's some reality where he made it home safely and opened his mechanic shop like he'd hoped to do. Where he and Marcus still get to ride around on horses in a big city.

"Do you think our timeline is very different from Manolo's? With your mom?" Jennie asks.

I sigh. "That's kind of hard to think about. Of course, I want my reality to be different from his. I want Mom to be with me forever."

My voice catches in my throat and Jennie lays her head back down on my shoulder.

I wonder if there's a reality where Jennie doesn't hide her pain about her dad under a mountain of words and snacks. If there's a world where Marcus's brain doesn't trick him into thinking he's still in danger.

We drive in silence until I see a sign that announces we've entered Santa Fe.

"Alvarez, you know we've got your back, right? No matter what happens," Marcus says, glancing at me and giving me a small smile.

Jennie squeezes my hand again. "Exactly. You're stuck with us. We are officially glued together in this timeline."

Marcus stops the truck at a four-way stop and I think about what Manolo told us. About how all the choices we're faced with each day create new realities and new timelines. Marcus could turn left or right or he could keep going straight. Whatever way he chooses would take us on a different path.

If I hadn't stolen the slushie machine, I would've been on a different path. And I'm not sure where this one will take me.

But as I hold on to Jennie's hand and watch Marcus head straight toward the airport, I know one thing.

I'm not on this journey alone. And whatever comes

across my path, even if it's orclings, blargmores, or worse, I'll be able to face it.

Because I'll have the rest of my traveling party by my side.

AUTHOR'S NOTE

IN THE SUMMER of 2019, my sister, Heather, asked if I wanted to go to Ghost Ranch, New Mexico, with her to work as the ranch librarian while she served as the wilderness medic. I lived in a run-down trailer with orange shag carpet, organized dusty books, and avoided green chilies in the dining hall.

From that experience, *The Ghosts of Rancho Espanto* was born.

All the lore surrounding Rancho Espanto is taken from the real history of Ghost Ranch. There really were outlaw brothers who spread stories of earth babies, monster snakes, and ghosts to scare people away from the area where they kept their stolen cattle. Once the Archuleta brothers died in the late 1800s, the land was later won in a card game by Roy Pfaffle. His wife, Carol Bishop Stanley, turned it into a riding resort after she claimed the ranch in her divorce from Roy. Eventually, the land was bought by Arthur Pack, an environmentalist who sold a tract of land to Georgia O'Keeffe, a famous painter who lived in a cabin at Ghost Ranch for several years. Many of her most popular paintings are inspired by the area. Arthur Pack and his wife, Phoebe, donated the land to the Presbyterian Church in 1955, and Ghost Ranch is now a nonprofit organization providing artistic, scientific, and spiritual workshops amid the stunning natural landscape.

Visiting Ghost Ranch helped me appreciate the hidden history in so many places we often take for granted. The places we walk by every day, the areas we don't give a second thought to. Underneath, there are stories rumbling, waiting to get out and be told.

Find them!

Organizing book donations at the Ghost Ranch library.

There were spiders waiting for me in half the boxes.

ACKNOWLEDGMENTS

JUST LIKE RAFA, I'm thankful to have my traveling party with me on this author journey. We've faced down our fair share of blargmores, and I can't think of a better group of people supporting me.

First, my agent, Stefanie Sanchez Von Borstel at Full Circle Literary, whose extrovert superpowers have supported me and lifted my career to heights I never expected. Thank you for your limitless encouragement. You are still the only person I willingly talk on the phone with.

My editor, Trisha de Guzman at FSG/Macmillan, is a warrior who scales rock walls and braves haunted cabins. You push me to improve and expand, lovingly helping me craft my stories into something more. I'm forever grateful for our partnership and friendship.

I owe a massive plate of quesitos to the entire team at Macmillan who champions my stories. Chantal Gersch and Kristen Luby work tirelessly on my behalf, protecting this introvert from actual social interaction.

Thank you to Abraham Matias for your incredible cover art and bringing Rancho Espanto to life. Thank you to book designer Samira Iravani.

I'm grateful to author friends Natalia Goldberg and Lori Keckler for letting me vent, scream, and celebrate in our never-ending chat. Sharing my joys and trials with you means so much.

Sarah Kapit will always have a place in my acknowledgments and in my heart for being my first critique partner and giving me the courage to embrace the title of "author." I love collaborating with you as we give other writers that same bravery.

Mi hermana de corazón, Amparo Ortiz, has been on the receiving end of more all-caps texts than I care to admit. I will scream about K-pop, books, and K-dramas with you forever. Thank you for your friendship and for being a part of my life.

My sister, Heather, spent a summer with me at Ghost Ranch, and I'm grateful she encouraged me to experience something new. Many thanks to my brother-in-law, Rob, for answering all my time-travel and wormhole questions. And to my mom and Lori Ragland for helping me with the horse information.

Joe and Soren, you are my whole heart. Any story I manage to put out in the world is due to your unwavering support and love, as well as your ability to answer my endless questions about the military, welding, and how to properly spell English words. Thank you for always being by my side, laughing with me, and celebrating every twist and turn along the way.

Finally, to my wonderful readers—thank you for journeying with me this far. Let's keep telling our stories and having new adventures!

ALSO BY ADRIANNA CUEVAS